ACTION HERO

THE FINCREDIBLE DIARY OF FIN SPENCER

Ciaran Murtagh is a writer of books and television programmes for children. Ciaran lives in London — to find out more about what he's writing and appearing in, follow him on Twitter @ciaranmurtagh or head over to

www.ciaranmurtagh.com

Books by Ciaran Murtagh

CHARLIE FLINT AND THE DINOS

Dinopants

Dinopoo

Dinoburps

Dinoball

BALTHAZAR THE GENIE

Genie in Training

Genie in Trouble

Genie in a Trap

THE FINCREDIBLE DIARY OF FIN SPENCER

Stuntboy

Rockstar

ACTION HERO
THE FINCREDIBLE DIARY OF FIN SPENCER

by CIARAN MURTAGH

with illustrations throughout by TIM WESSON

Piccadilly
PRESS

First published in Great Britain in 2016 by
Piccadilly Press
80-81 Wimpole Street, London, W1G 9RE
www.piccadillypress.co.uk

Text copyright © Ciaran Murtagh, 2016
Illustrations copyright © Tim Wesson, 2016

A CIP catalogue record for this book is available from the British Library.

ISBN: 978-1-848-12532-2
also available as an ebook

Printed and bound by Clays Lts, St Ives PLC

MIX
Paper from
responsible sources
FSC® C018072

Piccadilly Press is an imprint of Bonnier Zaffre,,
a Bonnier Publishing Company
www.bonnierpublishing.co.uk

To my Dad.
All Action, all Hero,
all the time

MONDAY

My name is Fin Spencer and I am in BIG trouble. Trouble so huge you can probably see it from the moon. Trouble so massive it makes Mount Everest look like a face pimple. Trouble so humungous I'm going to have to move to Australia, change my name to Billy Big Trouble and live inside a kangaroo.

Did I mention I'm in TROUBLE?

Luckily, I have a magic diary that might just be able to fix it. *This diary*. The only problem is that I promised NEVER to use it again. I meant it too! You see, the magic has a habit of backfiring. But I'm already in more trouble than a goldfish in a shark tank, so what have I got to lose?

Friends?

Besides, this time I'm going to be extra careful. There will be NO MISTAKES!

I <u>knew</u> today was going to be trouble as soon as I got in the shower. I'd barely started on my sixth soapy lathering when Mum shouted at me to get out! Apparently I was late and she thinks I spend too long getting ready in the morning. Doesn't she know that looking this good takes time?! And it doesn't help when you've run out of **Man Zest** shower gel. Thanks, Dad 'I splurge it on like spot cream' Spencer. Anyway, after she'd shouted at me for the fifth time

I got out of the shower, did my hair, pulled on my shirt, re-did my hair, pulled on my jumper, did my hair again — should probably leave that until last next time — and headed downstairs.

For once I was actually looking forward to school. It's nearly half term and Mrs Johnson has arranged for the whole class to go to the

Stevie Knuckles Action Adventure Camp

Stevie Knuckles is the bravest guy on TV and his camp sounds **AMAZING**. A week away from our parents while putting ourselves in brain-busting amounts of DANGER! Who knew Mrs Johnson would be ace enough to arrange something like that!? I always knew she had a *cool* bone in her body somewhere!

Last night Mum and Dad finally signed the form saying I could go, and handed over the cheque. At last I had my access all areas pass to a week of danger, peril and *barbecue food*!

Just in time too, because the form and cheque had to be handed in today. Mum and Dad had been keeping me in suspense for a whole week! They knew I'd do **ANYTHING** to make sure I didn't miss **Action Camp** and have really been making the most of it.

- Wash the car every Sunday? Check!
- Clean out my sock drawer? Check!
- Clean out my DAD'S sock drawer? Check! Check! Check!

I even had to help my little sister **ELLIE** with her 'artwork'. She's really into making collages at the moment, which as far as I can tell is just scribbling on a piece of paper and covering it in glitter and stickers. Don't get me started on the stickers. She's been sticking them to <u>EVERYTHING</u> — even me! Last week I went to school with a squashy foam love heart on my bum and didn't realise until I got stuck to my chair. **BRAD RADLEY** was first to notice. He made up a song about me that he sang all through lunchbreak:

**Fin Spencer
is so dumb!
Fin Spencer
loves his bum!
Everyone called them
Fin and Farter
And they lived
happily ever after!**

It's quite funny I suppose, but that's not the point. The point is I've earned this trip: I can't wait to meet **Stevie Knuckles**!

Stevie's the guy that gets dropped into the Amazon with nothing but a pencil sharpener, a pair of diving flippers and a potato masher and still manages to come out alive! He's handsome, brave and eats **a lot** of bugs. We could be twins. Apart from the bug-eating thing. Has he never heard of pizza delivery?!

Delivery for Mr Knuckles

At **Stevie's Action Camp** you spend a week in the wild learning how to be a real-life **Action Hero** just like him. It sounds right up my street or should that be **swamp?** I was <u>BORN</u> to be an **Action Hero** — bulging muscles, brilliant sense of humour, t-shirts with **weird** stains on them . . .

<u>I've got the lot!</u>

I'm destined for a life of danger, daring-do and **DEADLY SURVIVAL.** I mean, I already survive living with Mum and Dad, how much more deadly can it get?

With the end of term and **Action Camp** in sight, life should be good now, right?

WRONG!

15

When I got to class the form and cheque were MISSING! Panicking like a turkey in a Christmas shop, I emptied my bag onto my desk. I found a 5p coin that smelled of cheese, an **X-WING** badge I thought I'd swallowed and a pack of mouldy sandwiches that had been there <u>SO</u> long they'd turned into a new life form. But there was no form and no cheque.

Maybe the sandwiches had eaten them?

Or maybe, just maybe, I was in such a rush this morning that I forgot to pack them, and the key to my future happiness was still sat on the kitchen table at home . . .

I'm still blaming the sandwiches.

Today was our last chance to hand them in! I tried to reason with Mrs Johnson, but she wasn't having any of it. She said that I knew the deadline and if I wanted to leave everything until the last minute then that was MY FAULT. I tried to explain that I didn't want to leave everything until the last minute – my mum and dad did! – but Mrs Johnson wasn't listening. She said she was sorry, but there was nothing she could do. Which we all know is teacher-speak for, 'Suck it up, loser boy.'

At break-time I phoned Dad, but he was in a meeting. Then I called Mum but she didn't pick up either.

What would **Stevie Knuckles** do in this situation? Would **Stevie Knuckles** let something like a missing cheque ruin his **Action Hero** dreams?

Of course he wouldn't!

He'd race home, break in through the cat flap and grab that cheque right off the kitchen table! So that's what I was going to do . . . I raced down the corridor, gambolled past the watercooler and made my break for freedom.

I DIDN'T GET VERY FAR.

I had just put one foot outside the school door when Mr Finch, the headmaster, saw me. Trust me, if **Stevie Knuckles** had to get past Mr Finch every time he went on an expedition he'd never leave his bedroom.

Mr Finch asked me what I was doing. Leaving school grounds <u>without</u> permission was an immediate detention. I tried to laugh it off – technically only my foot had left the school grounds so I argued that only my foot should have detention. He wasn't having any of it – detention after school it was!

I was just telling **JOSH DOYLE** all about my bad luck when my best friend did something he'd <u>NEVER</u> done before. He had a good idea! He suggested I use a computer to fake the cheque and form and then just say I'd found it in my trouser pocket or something. It was perfect! After lunch we have ICT and I could use the school computers. Technically Mum and Dad had already given the cheque and form to me. Just because I didn't have them — or the sandwiches had eaten them — didn't mean they didn't want me to go.

I headed off to lunch with a **spring** in my step. A little too much of a **spring**, as it turned out, because when I got into the dinner hall I bumped into **CLAUDIA RONSON**

and spilled her lunch all over the floor.

DISASTER!

Although looking at the state of the school lunch I might just have saved her life . . .

CLAUDIA is the prettiest girl in the school and she's in my class too, along with **JOSH** and **BRAD RADLEY**. We're kind of boyfriend and girlfriend, but we're kind of not really, if you know what I mean. We've been on a couple of dates, which is pretty cool, but the last one didn't end well. We went to the cinema, you see. Who decided the cinema was a good place for a date? Two hours sitting in the dark not talking to each other — how is that romantic!? It didn't help that I let **CLAUDIA** pick the film . . .

ATTACK OF THE ZOMBIE PYTHONS

<u>I'm terrified of snakes!</u> But you don't admit that when you're on a date, do you? Especially not when you're an **Action Hero** like me. So when she re-enacted her favourite scene of **TERROR** from the trailer, I laughed and said, 'Call that scary? I eat snakes for breakfast.' Which we all know isn't true because I eat **COCO SNAPS!**

Anyway, I was just about keeping it together by closing my eyes at the REALLY SCARY bits — luckily I was wearing 3D glasses, so **CLAUDIA** didn't notice — until about halfway through when a great big python took me by surprise and leaped out of the screen towards me. I threw my hands in the air and screamed,

Not the face!

Unfortunately my glasses and popcorn went flying, and I knocked **CLAUDIA**'s drink all over her dress. She looked like some kind of weird lemonade-popcorn monster. Then she started to cry and ran out of the cinema.

We haven't spoken properly since. I was hoping being at **Action Camp** together would get me back in her good books, maybe even become officially boyfriend and girlfriend, but without the form and cheque there's no chance. And now I've spilled food all over her **AGAIN**.

Anyway, I have bigger things to worry about than **CLAUDIA** now, because in ICT things got worse. Just as I was trying to fake the cheque from my parents, **BRAD RADLEY** walked past and saw what I was doing. He gave me a 'you're for it now' smile and told Mrs Johnson what I was up to. She flipped out like a pancake at a pancake party. Did I know that forging a cheque was a crime? Answer: no. Apparently I could go to prison for it. Mrs Johnson didn't send me to prison, though, she sent me somewhere much worse. Mr Finch's office.

The good news was that I was out of detention, the bad news was that Mr Finch phoned Mum and asked her to come and take me home for being 'deceitful'. Mum was so **angry** her glasses fogged up as she was driving and she nearly crashed the car FIVE times — and apparently that was my fault too!

When Dad got home he was just as **angry**. I tried to explain, but they wouldn't listen! Mum and Dad banned me from **Action Camp** which as a punishment was a bit dumb because I couldn't go anyway, that's why I'd been trying to fake the form! The **weird** thing was that the cheque and form weren't on the table where I thought I'd left them last night.

Where had they got to?

When Mum collected **ELLIE** from school, I found out. She'd been given a merit for her latest piece of 'art'. Surprise, surprise it was a collage — made out of my cheque and form! She had carefully snipped them into little triangles to make a picture she'd called 'Hope'. When I saw it I was so angry I wanted to rearrange her face into a Picasso! Dad popped it on the fridge with a magnet. Mum was on **ELLIE**'s side too. She had told her to take some scrap paper from the table this morning, and apparently if I spent less time getting ready in the mornings then none of this would have happened.

Just when I think things can't get any worse, Mum has an idea. Now that I'm not going to Action Camp she thinks it would be good to go on a family holiday to Aunt Tabitha's in Scotland . . .

Nooooooooooooooooooooooo!

The last time we visited Aunt Tabitha it rained every day, we ate nothing but porridge and she made me wear a kilt. Yep, that's right, **A WOOLLEN SKIRT**. It was so windy that every time we went to the shops I showed my pants! The butcher even started calling me **Flasher Fin**. It could have been worse — at least there wasn't a love heart stuck to my bum — but I can't go back there. **EVER**.

So that's why I need to use the diary. Right now I'm banned from **Action Camp**, and am facing two weeks up a freezing mountain in a skirt.

Things couldn't be any worse!

We all remember the diary rules, right?

FIN SPENCER'S
FINCREDIBLE
DIARY RULES

1. The diary only changes the things I say and do or wished I'd said and done

2. It only changes things if I write about what I wish I'd done **ON THE DAY** they happen

3. Diaries are still for `losers`. It's only this one that's cool.

If I can change today, it should all be fine.

I just need to make sure I got out of the shower extra early this morning and put the letter and cheque safely into my schoolbag before **ELLIE** got downstairs. And, while I'm at it, maybe I could make sure I didn't bump into **CLAUDIA** in the lunch hall . . .

Are you listening, diary?

Up early and no spilled lunch — in fact I was extra careful when I went into the canteen and even gave **CLAUDIA** a bag of crisps.

I'm counting on you, diary - a week in the wild getting close to nature, and maybe even **CLAUDIA RONSON**, depends on you!

TUESDAY

As soon as I woke up this morning I ran downstairs to look at the fridge door. Don't worry, it's not some crazy new hobby I'm into, I just wanted to see if the diary had worked.

The good news was that 'Hope' had gone, which meant my cheque and form must have made it to school instead — result! The bad news was that the collage had been replaced by a different one. **ELLIE** had cut up an old photo of me, a chocolate bar wrapper, some old material and a page from one of her books, so whatever it was had my face, seven eyes, a unicorn's horn and Postman Pat's body! It also seemed to really like Fudgetastical chocolate bars. Sometimes I worry about my sister. No, scratch that, I **ALWAYS** worry about my sister.

There was a big arrow pointing to the creature's face with the word 'Fin' scrawled next to it. I was about to 'hide' it in the bin when Mum came downstairs and told me to go for my shower.

Get in the shower, get OUT of the shower — I wish she'd make her mind up!

In the shower, the Man Zest hadn't been replaced. Instead I had to use Mum's

Magnolia Marvel stuff that she got from Aunt Tabitha for Christmas. When I got out I smelled like a **pensioner's hankie!** I complained to Mum about it over breakfast but she said that she's not wasting money on more shower gel until all the stuff we've got has gone, even if it does make everyone smell like an **explosion in a flower shop.**

At school **CLAUDIA RONSON** was waiting for me by the main door and at first I was worried. But then I remembered that the diary had worked for the collage so it should have worked for knocking her dinner tray too . . . and when I got close she handed me a sweet to say thank you for the crisps I gave her yesterday.

Score!

The only problem was that it was a Choco Chew. Now, I like almost all kinds of chocolate, but if there's one thing I hate it's Choco Chews – they taste like a troll's welcome mat! The chewy bits get stuck in your teeth and make everything taste of day-old chocolate. I couldn't say that, though, because it'd be rude and **CLAUDIA** is finally talking to me again for the first time in ages, so I popped it in my pocket and told her I'd eat it 'later', which we all know is Fin-speak for 'NEVER.'

In class Mrs Johnson was pleased to announce that the whole class was going to Action Camp on Friday – even me!

(Thank you, diary! I don't know what I was worried about, I've clearly got the hang of this thing now.)

Even better: because we were all going Mr Finch had agreed that Mrs Johnson could use some class time to help us prepare. **BRILLIANT!** School is practically over. Today and tomorrow we're doing **Action Camp** training and on Thursday Mrs Johnson always lets us bring in games to play anyway — result!

The only person not smiling was **CLIFF SHRAPNEL**. This was because now that the whole class was definitely going to camp, Mrs Johnson had to bring in some extra help — and **CLIFF**'s dad had volunteered to come with us.

Unlucky!

I can't think of **ANYTHING** more embarrassing.

CLIFF plays guitar in my band **System of the Future** – it's the coolest band in the school. (OK it's the ONLY band in the school, but that still counts.) Anyway, at lunch we practised a new song and I tried to be sympathetic about the whole 'Dad going to **Action Camp**' thing but I can't help but laugh – whoever heard of an **Action Hero** going on adventures with their dad? Unfortunately **CLIFF** didn't see the funny side of it and stormed off. That was the end of band practice. **Some people have no sense of humour!**

After break Mrs Johnson showed us **Action Camp**'s website on the whiteboard. It looked <u>even better</u> than I remembered. There's rock climbing, rafting, bungee-jumping . . . **My muscles were rippling at the thought!** Then things got even better. Mrs Johnson told us that while we were at the camp we were all entered into a competition. There will be a leaderboard and we'll be awarded points for all the activities we take part in. Then the boy or girl at the top of the leaderboard at the end of the week will get a trophy and be named **Action Hero of The Week**. Brilliant! Best of all, our class **Action Hero** will be given the trophy by . . . **Stevie Knuckles** himself. How cool is that? **I have to win!**

Before I know it **Stevie Knuckles**
will be inviting me along on his most dangerous
adventures! We'll be diving into jungle caves
and bungee-jumping with killer whales by

Christmas. I'll finally be famous! I'll be rich! I'll be the **Action Hero** I always knew I was!

Then Mrs Johnson brings me back to reality with a bump — it's time for my worst subject: <u>GEOGRAPHY</u>. She says she's going to 'break out the action maps' and continue our 'camp training', but when she brings out the same dusty old maps we always use I realise we've been conned. You don't make something cool just by putting the word 'action' in front of it. Whoever heard of an **Action Hero** with a map anyway? **Action Heroes** find their way by studying broken twigs and animal poo. So instead I spend the time planning out all the adventures **Stevie** and I are going to have on TV!

Unfortunately Mrs Johnson didn't mention that there was going to be a test. **JOSH** gets ten out of ten and Mrs Johnson crowns him her **Action Hero**. I get nothing right and **BRAD RADLEY** calls me an **Action ZERO**. Before I know it the rest of the class are laughing and calling me it too. I've just got a new nickname —

If **Stevie Knuckles** finds out we'll NEVER go white-water rafting with sabretooth penguins!

Things get even worse when **BRAD RADLEY** notices that I smell like a granny's garden — not helping! **Action Heroes**

don't smell of flowers, but **Action ZEROs** might . . .

I NEED TO USE THE DIARY AGAIN.

When I get home I'm about to rush upstairs when I notice **ELLIE** has been doing more of her 'artwork'. This time she's been using my superhero comics! She shows me a new superhero she's invented — Super Spider Banjo Woman. I can't quite believe my eyes!

She's given Superman the legs of Wonder Woman, the face of a spider and the body of a banjo from her PRINCESS TWINKLE MAGIC CASTLE fan club magazine. PRINCESS TWINKLE is the most annoying character on TV. She's best friends with a magic toaster and a spoon called Nigel and for some reason **ELLIE** loves her! Mum thinks the collage is 'very creative', which is Mum-speak for 'rubbish but I can't say so'.

Mum has no sympathy about my comics. Apparently she's been telling me to move them out of the way all week. I rush into the lounge and carry what's left of my collection up to my bedroom before **ELLIE** can attack them any more.

The only thing that cheers me up is the

thought of **ELLIE** freezing her bum off at Aunt Tabitha's while I'm living the life of an **Action Hero** with **Stevie Knuckles**, but even that doesn't last long. At dinner **ELLIE** says that she doesn't think it's fair that I get to have a cool holiday while she has to go all the way to boring Scotland. It seems that Dad agrees with her. He says, 'It is an awfully long way.' Which we all know is Dad-speak for 'I'd rather stay on the sofa and scratch my bum.'

Mum sighs and gets out the laptop and before Dad can say anything she's booked them all a trip to . . . PRINCESS TWINKLE'S MAGIC FAIRY LAND! **ELLIE** is thrilled. Dad looks like he's just swallowed a chainsaw. I try not to laugh – bad luck, Dad!

After dinner I settle down on the sofa for a **Stevie Knuckles** marathon. If I want to be an **Action Hero** just like him, then I need to find out more about the man himself.

It seems there's nothing he can't do:

- Make an igloo – Check!
- Navigate a rainforest – Check!
- Skin a large rat and eat its brains with a stick – er, WHY WOULD YOU WANT TO DO THAT!?

Maybe when I meet him I can introduce him to the wonders of burger bars and Chinese takeaways. But I'm NEVER going to impress him if my nickname is **Action ZERO** so it's time to get to work.

Diary, are you listening?

This afternoon I studied the map harder than anyone else, aced the test and took my first step towards becoming the **Action Hero** we all know I am. While we're at it, this morning I got up early and moved ALL my superhero comics to my bedroom. Super Spider Banjo Woman is NOT a thing and NEVER will be!

I'm starting to realise how much I've missed this diary – it's brilliant! I think I'm going to keep writing in it at **Action Camp**. That way when I'm rich and famous on TV eating an elephant's eyeball, kids can read this book to find out how I made it.

No need to thank me – you're welcome!

WEDNESDAY

When I woke up this morning my comics were all in one piece and piled up on my desk — result! I'm so relieved I spend half an hour flicking through the best ones and I'm late going for my shower — oops!

When I get into the bathroom Mum has gone overboard on the shower gel. She's put out every shower gel Aunt Tabitha has <u>ever</u> given her.

❀ Magnolia Marvel ❀

❀ Lavender Lovely ❀

❀ Primrose Promenade ❀

I don't want to use any of them — I'm an **Action Hero**! — but the sooner I get rid of them the sooner Mum will buy me some more **Man Zest**. So I bravely take a splurge from each and mix it all together. Unfortunately mixing them all together does something to the chemicals and soon my arm pits are burning! After a shorter-than-usual shower I spend breakfast with two cold flannels up my jumper trying to soothe my burning skin! The day hasn't started well.

At school **CLAUDIA** is waiting for me with another Choco Chew. This is bad! I can't say I don't like them now because I took one yesterday and said I loved them. If I come clean she'll think I'm a liar but I'm not, I'm a hero! So I do the only thing I can and shove the sweet in my pocket with the other one from yesterday. I wish she'd buy me something different, I'd rather eat ANYTHING but a Choco Chew — even a spinach sandwich! The TV advert has a really annoying jingle that gets stuck in your head too . . .

Choco Chews! Choco Chews!
Choco Chews **are good for you!**
Choco Chews, **nothing else will do!**
Everyone loves Choco Chews!

I don't!

In fact I hate them so much I've made up my own rhyme to sing at the TV whenever the advert comes on.

Choco Chews! Choco Chews!
The only chew that tastes of poo!
Choco Chews **will make you spew!**
Eat one and you'll need the loo!

Much *better!* I wouldn't touch a Choco Chew if I was starving to death. It's unfortunate that the love of my life keeps giving them to me.

Before we head into class **CLAUDIA** takes a big sniff and says

You smell nice.

She wants to know what shower gel I'm using. Quietly I tell her it's a special mix of *Lavender Lovely, Magnolia Marvel* and *Primrose Promenade* but just as I'm saying that **BRAD RADLEY** walks past and laughs so hard his face turns purple.

We spend the morning pitching tents on the sports field. It's 'practice' apparently, but I don't know how much it'll help us because they're not even the tents we're going to take to **Action Camp**, but ones the Scouts keep in the games cupboard at school. **JOSH** and I team up with **CLIFF** and get to work. It's harder than it looks, and I didn't think it looked easy!

The only person not bothering to do anything is **BRAD RADLEY**. He's got a

49

really cool pop-up tent that he's brought in to show off to everyone. It's so unfair, he just throws it in the air and it pops into shape like some kind of futuristic Frisbee. While the rest of us are struggling with tent poles and guy ropes **BRAD** just sits back and watches.

I get *so angry* trying to figure out which one of the ropes is called 'Guy' that I accidentally hit **JOSH**'s thumb with a hammer! He screams like a four-year-old on a ghost train and Mrs Johnson comes over to see. She sends **JOSH** to see the nurse and gives me a very nasty look. It's not my fault! **JOSH** shouldn't have put his thumb where the hammer was going to be! Besides as far as I can tell I've actually done him a favour. While he's off having a biscuit with the school nurse **CLIFF** and I are left to do all the hard work!

We try our best, and when we're finished we step back to have a look. It's not good. It looks like an explosion on a washing line. If I were going on a camping adventure I think I'd rather sleep in a hedge.

Just then **JOSH** comes back with his thumb bandaged so much it looks like he's trying to hitch a lift on a spaceship.

He doesn't look impressed with our efforts and when he tugs at the tent zip, the whole thing comes tumbling down. Thanks, **JOSH**. Luckily the bell goes for lunch before I get

really angry!

Lunch is a shepherd's pie so bad it tastes like it's been made out of REAL SHEPHERDS. I force down as much as I can and then give up.

Just before home time Mrs Johnson gives us a list of all the things we need to bring with us on the trip. It's longer than a six-year-old's letter to Santa. Luckily it's late-night shopping at the mall so Mum sends me off with Dad to get everything.

When Dad sees the size of the list he decides it's time for me to 'take some personal responsibility' which we all know is **Dad-speak** for 'You shop while I have a coffee'. He tells me to call him when I'm ready for the checkout. **Result!** Dad is giving me free reign of the camping shop! I can pick whatever I want and nobody's going to stop me.

The first thing I want is a pop-up tent like **BRAD**'s. **CHECK**. Then I grab a top of the range sleeping bag, a ground sheet with built-in wifi speakers and a Swiss Army knife with over 108 **different functions** including:

1. KNIFE
2. MAGNIFYING GLASS
3. MINI SAW
4. EMERGENCY CAKE
5. INFLATABLE SAUSAGE

OK, I made those last two up but you get the idea. When I got to the checkout my trolley was piled **higher than a bodybuilder's dinner plate**! I called Dad to come and pay. By the time he got into the shop, the till was beeping **faster than an 80s computer game.**

When the final total appeared on the screen there were more zeros than a

Britain's Got Talent audition! Dad nearly had a heart attack. Then he had one of his brainwaves.

He tells the guy on the till that we don't need any of this stuff because he's just remembered he's got most of it packed away in the shed from when he was a boy. He cannot be serious! That was over a thousand years ago! The stuff is going to be PREHISTORIC! I don't want a **Stone Age sleeping bag!**

As we put everything back on the shelves I start to moan. I've got to have at least one new thing! So Dad caves and buys me the Swiss Army knife — result!

When we get home Dad takes me out into the shed. At the very back, behind a tin of paint that Dad keeps 'just in case' and

a spider so big it looks like it swallowed a cat, Dad finds a battered old cardboard box with the words 'Camping Gear' scrawled on the side.

Inside there's a tatty tent, a mouldy sleeping bag and a groundsheet covered in slug trails. Everything smells like socks. Dad HAS to take me back to the shop to buy new stuff now, right? WRONG!

Instead he says

It just needs a good airing

I was hoping that was Dad- speak for 'burned on a fire'. Sadly, it's not.

We shake everything out before hanging it on the washing line and by the time we're finished our garden looks like slug-aggedon! Dad sprays everything with the hose and I'm hoping it'll disintegrate under the pressure. No such luck. We leave it there to dry overnight.

Diary, you need to fix this!

If I turn up at **Stevie Knuckles' Action Adventure Camp** looking like I found my camping gear in a bin I'll be a laughing stock! Dad has to go back to the camping shop and buy me everything I want. **Action Heroes** don't go camping in tents that smell of socks. **Action Heroes** don't go camping in tents at all, but that's not the point! **You have to help me.**

THURSDAY

When I woke up all of Dad's camping gear was still on the line looking worse than ever. It had rained in the night and a bird had pooed on the sleeping bag — PERFECT.

The diary **HADN'T WORKED**. I didn't understand! There should have been a load of top camping stuff piled in the corner of my bedroom. Then I remembered, **the diary only changes things that I say and do.**

Last night I'd tried to change things my dad had done. I was so desperate to get what I wanted I'd <u>forgotten the most important rule</u> and now it's too late! Maybe **BRAD** was right and I am an **Action ZERO** . . .

To cheer myself up I had a play with my Swiss Army knife. As I fiddled with it this **weird** little hook popped out. I had no idea what it was for.

1. Catching tiny fish
2. A cockroach backscratcher
3. Snagging hard-to-reach bogies

Probably all three! I'm sure I'll find out eventually.

As I went downstairs I caught a glimpse of my camping gear through the window again.

It looked like it had just survived **a music festival in a war zone**. I didn't want to go on the trip at all if I had to take **THAT** lot. (And after what happened today that might be a very real possibility anyway, but we'll get to that.)

The only thing that cheered me up was the fact that it was technically the last day of term and that meant one thing – **games**! I'd been so caught up in the shopping trip that I'd nearly forgotten. I raced back upstairs and picked out the coolest game I own – Cosmic Kick Ball Carnage! You flick tiny footballs around a board and knock over aliens. It's brilliant. Mum and Dad got it for me for my birthday along with a really embarrassing pair of cartoon

Postman Pat pants that I keep only for emergencies.

I was just about to step outside the front door when Mum stopped me. She wanted to know where I was going with my new game. What was she talking about? The game wasn't new! My birthday was AGES ago, but mums' brains don't work like that. Apparently it was 'too good' to take to school, which we all know is Mum-speak for 'Put it down, loser boy!' She rummaged in the hall cupboard and came out holding the lamest game EVER – Marble Madness. It's rubbish. You basically have to make a tower out of sticks and run a marble down them. I grew out of it when I was four, around the same time I grew out of pants with Postman Pat on them!

Anyway, she wanted me to take it to school. I would rather have taken a dead cat. Turn up with Cosmic Kick Ball Carnage and I'm a hero, turn up with Marble Madness and I'm a bigger loser than Lionel Loser from Loserville. However it seemed I had no choice in the matter.

I stuffed it in my bag and stamped down the path. I would just have to keep it hidden away and play with everybody else's games.

At school CLAUDIA was waiting for me with ANOTHER Choco Chew! This is getting ridiculous — she's obsessed with the things. I really wanted to tell her I don't like them, but I've already lied twice. Instead I shoved it in my pocket with the

other two and told her

I'm saving it for a special occasion.

Like the day my tastebuds melt or when I want to poison myself before a maths test.

The rest of the morning is brilliant. I manage to keep **Marble Madness** out of sight and play with everybody else's games. The only person not having fun is **JOSH**. His mum rebandaged his thumb when he got home and added a sling — talk about overkill! He looks like he just came second in a fight with a lion.

CLIFF brought in NUCLEAR BATTLESHIPS. It's the second best game there is after Cosmic Kick Ball Carnage so I organised a whole class tournament. By lunchtime it's down to me and **BRAD RADLEY**. **CLIFF** declares a grand final after lunch. I'm so excited I can't eat, which is just as well as the dinner ladies are serving up toad-in-the-hole that looks like it's fresh from the pond.

After lunch the whole class gather round to witness me destroy **BRAD** at NUCLEAR BATTLESHIPS. He picked the wrong guy to mess with — I am **BRILLIANT** at this game. Mrs Johnson can't see what all the fuss is about and heads off to get a cup of coffee. It's all over in five minutes — I sink his battleship with a nuclear torpedo. Game over. **BRAD** isn't happy. He starts to sulk. I do a little victory dance, which just makes **BRAD** even angrier.

He says that at least he brought in a game, I didn't even do that. He calls me a 'sponger'. I tell him I'm not a sponger, I brought a game but . . .

The words are out of my mouth before I realise what I'm saying and **BRAD** is marching to my bag to see what I've got. I try to stop him but it's too late. He already has **Marble Madness** in his hand and is waving it in the air. He calls me a

massive loser

and everybody starts to laugh. I try to wrestle the game back off him but **BRAD** won't let go and before I know it the box has broken and marbles are flying across the floor.

Just then Mrs Johnson comes back in

with her cup of coffee. She slips on the marbles and goes **FLYING**. We watch as she crashes into her desk as if in slow motion.

She ends up crumpled on the floor with a coffee cup on her head. The only way I know she's not dead is because she's giving me the **dirtiest look I've ever seen.**

I rush over to try and help. I take my hankie from my pocket to mop up some of the coffee and three Choco Chews bounce off her forehead. Nightmare! When **CLAUDIA** sees the sweets she gets a bit upset. She thought I liked Choco Chews so why haven't I eaten them yet? Before I have a chance to explain Mrs Johnson asks someone to fetch the school nurse.

The nurse is worried and decides to send Mrs Johnson to hospital for suspected concussion. While we're waiting for the ambulance I try to pick up all the marbles. The whole class are staring at me like I'm some kind of teacher murderer and **CLAUDIA** is giving me the worst stare of all. We're NEVER going to be boyfriend and girlfriend now!

To make matters worse, Mr Finch has to take over Mrs Johnson's lessons. He's **so angry** that he makes us put all the games away and have a pop quiz on everything we've learned this term. If the class were staring at me angrily before, now they're looking at me like **I just punched Father Christmas!**

Lo and behold, just when I think things can't get any worse, **they do**.

Mr Finch gets a call from the hospital telling him that Mrs Johnson is going to have to stay in overnight, and when she gets out she's going to have to take it easy. This means no **Stevie Knuckles Action Adventure Camp**, which spells only one thing.

DISASTER!

Apparently this is all my fault too! I try to look for a friendly face in the classroom, but there isn't one. As soon as the bell rings I'm out of school **faster** than a leopard in a Lamborghini.

When I get home I tell Mum what happened and all she can talk about is **Marble Madness**— typical! Apparently she knew whatever game I took to school would get ruined, and aren't I glad I left Cosmic Kick Ball Carnage at home now? Why do parents **NEVER** get it?! If I'd taken Cosmic Kick Ball Carnage to school then **NONE** of this would have happened and we'd all still be going on the trip tomorrow!

Mum says she knows exactly what to do, and for a minute I think she's going to come up with the perfect solution. <u>I couldn't have been more wrong</u>. Instead she makes a quick call to PRINCESS TWINKLE'S MAGIC FAIRY LAND to see if they can squeeze me in. Apparently they can so long as I don't

71

mind sharing a bed with my sister.

If ever I've needed a magic diary in my life it's **NOW**. I race upstairs, and here I am. So, diary, are you listening? This morning I made it out of the door with Cosmic Kick Ball Carnage safely in my bag before Mum even knew what was happening, OK? That way Mrs Johnson would still have both her ankles in working order, I wouldn't be the monster who ruined the class holiday and, even better, I would have had **NO** reason to shower my teacher in Choco Chews, so **CLAUDIA** wouldn't be upset. You have to do this for me, diary. If you don't I'm going to have to move to San Francisco and disguise myself as a lamp-post!

FRIDAY

This morning I was scared to open my eyes. Either my life was still a disaster area or I was about to go on the holiday of a lifetime. It all depended on the diary. When I saw my rucksack packed at the end of the bed I breathed a sigh of relief. The trip to **Stevie Knuckles' Action Adventure Camp** was back on!

Thank you, diary!

Mum, Dad and **ELLIE** drove me to school to get on the coach. **Nothing** could stop me now! Turned out I was wrong. When we got out of the car, everyone was standing by the coach giving me evil looks. I didn't understand.

The diary had fixed everything, right?

WRONG!

Remember how I said the diary had a habit of backfiring on me? It had just done it AGAIN.

JOSH took me to one side and explained. Apparently I had taken Cosmic Kick Ball Carnage into school yesterday and got a little carried away in a particularly close game with **CLIFF**. I'd flicked the ball so hard it had got wedged up his nose.

I tried not to laugh but I couldn't help it. Poor **CLIFF** had a miniature football stuck up his nose! It sounded uncomfortable but not life-threatening, so why was everybody still staring at me? Well, it turns out **CLIFF** tried to dig the ball out with his finger and shoved it further up so now it needs to be surgically removed. I tried not to laugh again, but COME ON – this is funny! Why isn't anybody else laughing? Then **JOSH** told me that because **CLIFF** is having an operation his dad had just told everyone he's staying behind, so we don't have the extra adult we need. The trip's off. And it's all my fault. **AGAIN!**

Just when I think things can't get any worse, they do. MY dad agrees to go instead! It makes sense because it's his ticket out of a week of hell in PRINCESS TWINKLE'S MAGIC FAIRY LAND. He NEVER wanted to go in the first place! He hops in the car and heads back home to fetch his bag while everyone else gets on the coach. Now Dad's a hero and I feel like the biggest loser ever. Is it better to go to **Action Camp** with your dad for a week or be hated by your friends forever? It's a close call. In the end, Dad coming along just about wins.

Mum has driven Dad back to meet us, so eventually he clambers on the coach and sits down the front by the driver and Mrs Johnson. Mum is really sad he won't be joining her and **ELLIE** at PRINCESS TWINKLE'S MAGIC FAIRY LAND but agrees it's a good idea. She starts to cry as she says goodbye and gives Dad a **massive snog** in front of everyone! They make a sound like an eel being sucked up a vacuum. It's disgusting! She sniffs back a tear, points at me and says

My little soldier's all grown up.

Behind me **BRAD RADLEY** sniggers and says 'little soldier' under his breath.

I think I'd rather be called **Action Zero**. This coach can't get going fast enough.

ᴡᴡᴡ

I sit next to **JOSH** for the eight-hour trip to **Action Camp**. I plan to show him some videos on my phone and play him the latest **X-WING** album but **JOSH** has other ideas. It turns out he gets travel sick so instead he wants me to hold a plastic sick bag for him 'just in case'.

CLAUDIA sits opposite. It seems the diary worked on the whole Choco Chew thing too because she breaks out a bumper bag of them 'for the journey'. I smile and say thank you, maybe after lunch. Which is Fin-speak for 'In your dreams!'

Just when I think it can't get any worse **JOSH** falls asleep on my shoulder and starts to dribble. It's like being headbutted by a soggy dog! So I do the only thing I can do. I pop in my earphones and listen to *X-WING*.

I must have dropped off because when I woke up we were in a service station and there was a lake of drool on my shoulder — thank you, **JOSH**! At least he wasn't sick on me, I suppose.

We all headed into the service station for burgers. Because Dad's here and he's got loads more cash than anyone else I order the triple mega double burger with extra cheese. It's the biggest thing on the menu and looks like it could feed the entire coach. **Perfect.**

By the time I'm finished I'm feeling fuller than an *elephant's swimming trunks.*

Luckily the only thing I have to do is sit on a coach and have another nice long snooze.

Turns out that isn't going to happen.

Just as I'm settling down for the next four hours of the journey **CLAUDIA** leans over and offers me the bumper bag of Choco Chews saying,

I hope you left room for dessert!

I haven't left room for anything, apart from maybe a heart attack. I try to fob her off but she isn't having any of it. She laughs and says, 'Anyone would think you don't even *like* Choco Chews.' This is too close to the truth for my comfort, so I take one to keep her quiet and she watches me unwrap it. I have <u>no</u> choice but to pop it into my mouth.

It tastes worse than I remember. It's like chewing a ferret's football boot. I do my best to make it look like I'm enjoying it, but it's tough! I just about manage to swallow it down. Eventually **CLAUDIA** plugs in her earphones and closes her eyes and I breathe a sigh of relief. But not for long. My stomach is gurgling like a plughole and the taste of MY OWN BREATH makes me feel like I want to puke! **JOSH** sees what's about to happen and holds open the sick bag.

He's just in time and soon I'm holding a warm bag of sick. Way to go, Action Hero!

Luckily no one but **JOSH** has noticed. I have to get rid of it before anyone does notice! There's a little toilet down the back, so I take the bag in there and flush it down the loo.

It's then that my day gets even worse. The bag must have clogged the loo because the toilet immediately starts to overflow. I don't know what to do! I run out of the toilet and a river of toilet water follows me down the coach like a poo tsunami!

Soon everyone's noticed what's happened and the driver pulls over. He wants to know who blocked the loo. I raise my hand and try to explain but nobody's listening. We spend **TWO HOURS** on the hard shoulder while the coach company sends someone to unblock the loo and give the coach a good clean. Even my dad looks embarrassed to be with me.

Because we spent so long on the hard shoulder we got stuck in rush-hour traffic and the journey took even longer. By the time we got to **Stevie Knuckles' Action Adventure Camp** it was too dark to put up the tents and everyone on the coach was ready to sacrifice me to the Inca gods.

Luckily the camp has some log cabins, so we're given a cold dinner and sent to bed. Just as everyone's dropping off to sleep I sneak out the diary. I don't want to start **Action Camp** as the boy who got sick on the bus and flooded a loo! To be honest, I don't want to start **Action Camp** as the boy who's got his dad with him either but there's nothing I can do about that. Nostril-ball happened yesterday and I can't use the diary to change Dad's mind about coming. I can only change what I did today, and I shouldn't have flushed the bag down the loo.

Dear diary, please make that happen — this Action Hero's counting on you.

SATURDAY

This morning I'm woken by a stink so bad I think my nose is going to melt. It smells like a *skunk* has had an argument with a *nappy* in a *sewer*. I don't have to look very far to find out where it's coming from.

Buried in the bottom of my rucksack is **A BAG OF COLD SICK**. It seems I didn't flush the bag down the loo after all — RESULT.

Almost. Instead, I put it inside my rucksack and now everything I own smells of triple mega double burger sick! GROSS! I shove two bits of toilet paper up my nose and carry the bag outside. It's early, so I don't think anyone else noticed.

I chuck the sick bag in a bin and head back. I open a few windows to get rid of the smell and pretend I've only just woken up myself. I do a big yawn and then notice everyone is looking at me really weirdly. Dad whispers,

Fin, you've got toilet paper up your nose.

BUSTED!

I whip it out double-quick and make up some excuse about hay fever. I grab my wash bag and head for the shower block. Way to go, **Action Hero**!

In the shower block **BRAD RADLEY** asks how the 'little soldier' slept and I decide to ignore him. I tip my wash bag onto the bench and freeze. Mum has put a big bottle of *Magnolia Marvel* in there with a little note stuck to it saying, **I know this is your favourite!**

When **BRAD** sees this he rushes off to tell everyone else. Thanks, Mum.

I hop in the shower and turn on the tap. The water is **colder than a penguin's bottom**. Seriously, if it was any colder it would be coming out as ice cubes. Luckily this means I don't have time to use the *Magnolia Marvel* shower gel. I give myself a quick rinse and hop out to get changed.

I pull on my clothes and try to do something with my hair. It's not looking good. I throw on some gel and try to flatten it. When my brush gets stuck for the fifth time I realise I'm going to have to live with it. When I catch sight of myself in the mirror I shudder. My hair looks like a badger's twig wig! I shove on a baseball cap and hope no one notices.

Popular badger wigs of the 21st Century

After breakfast, **LANCE**, the camp leader, calls us into the Welcome Circle, which is **LANCE**-speak for 'bit of grass'. **LANCE** is hunkier than a bodybuilding buffalo.

When he smiles it looks like he's swallowed a piano. I hate him already!

The first thing **LANCE** wants to know is whether anyone's been to a **Stevie Knuckles' Action Adventure Camp** before. Everybody shakes their head, but then **BRAD** nudges me in the back and makes me take a step forward. **LANCE** thinks I'm telling him that I have been before and flashes me a smile that's brighter than the sun.

'Cool!' he says. 'So you know the **Stevie Knuckles Salute**, right?'

But before I have a chance to reply **LANCE** starts to demonstrate.

It looks like he's trying to land a jumbo jet while swatting a fly at a disco. I have no idea what he's doing, but everybody's looking at me, so I try and join in.

I wave my hands about like a **toddler in a swimming pool** and do my best to copy **LANCE**. Just when I think I'm getting into it **LANCE** does a quick flick that I'm not expecting and bops me on the nose. I fall to the floor. **LANCE** is quick to apologise but the damage is done. I tell him it's OK, but my nose is swelling up and what comes out sounds more like:

Dit's Doh-K!

I sound like **a duck with a head cold!**

I go to the loo to dab on some cold water and in the mirror I can see my nose turning bright red. **BRILLIANT**. It looks like my face just hosted a hornet hoe down.

When I get back to the Welcome Circle **CLAUDIA** is talking to her friends. I overhear her say she thinks **LANCE** is 'really cool!' What is she talking about? Didn't she just see him beat up her boyfriend!? Sometimes I just don't understand girls.

Just then Dad arrives from the cabin. He's been getting changed into his **Action Hero** gear and suddenly I wish **LANCE** had poked out my eyes as well as bopping me on the nose. Dad's wearing very short shorts, a tie-dye t-shirt and a bandana. What's he wearing a bandana for? He hasn't even got any hair!

LANCE smiles and says Dad looks 'a million dollars', which is clearly **LANCE**-speak for 'a total twazzock'! He asks Dad to come out front and help him unveil the leaderboard.

It's in the centre of the circle and **LANCE** and Dad whip off the sheet that covers it. Underneath there's an old tree trunk. Part of the trunk's been replaced by a blackboard. One by one we all have to write our names on the board. While we're doing this **LANCE** explains how it works: we get points for every activity we complete at Action Camp and the person with the most points at the end of the week gets a trophy from **Stevie Knuckles.**

Just as I'm writing down my name **BRAD**

sticks up his hand and asks if there's a loser board just for Fin Spencer and whether I get points for the girliest shower gel. I'm in no mood for **BRAD**. I say 'very funny' but it comes out as 'derry dunny', which just makes matters worse.

As we're heading back to the cabin I tell **JOSH** I'm going to win this thing ('din dis ding') but **BRAD RADLEY** overhears and says he NEVER heard of an Action Hero whose dad comes with him on the camp. I tell him I am an Action Hero ('daction dero') and to prove it I show him my Swiss Army knife. The little hook thing pops out again and **BRAD** laughs — very impressive!

What's it for anyway?

1. A tiny hook for tiny pirates

2. A toenail cleaner

3. A gerbil's bum scratcher . . . ?

I still have absolutely no idea!

We spend the rest of the day putting up our tents. Dad and Mrs Johnson are sleeping in the log cabin with **LANCE** so Dad offers to help put mine up. I tell him I don't need any help but Dad isn't listening. He picks up a mallet and pegs and gets to work. When **LANCE** sees what's happening he calls me out for cheating and takes off some points before I even start earning any! I try to explain that I didn't want my dad to help me but thanks to my nose I sound like a goose in a traffic jam. **LANCE** nods and puts the points back on because I wasn't cheating but takes more points off for being a bad team player. **I give up!** I tell Dad to just stay away from me for the rest of the camp.

When I'm finished things don't get any better. My tent looks like it's just survived a hurricane. It's worse than last time. I do my best to straighten it out but it only makes things worse. This **Action Hero** stuff is harder than it looks.

JOSH takes pity on me and says I can share his tent if I want. As I'm already in negative points on the leaderboard for 'bad team player' I don't think things can get any more terrible so I'm happy to agree.

I crawl into **JOSH**'s tent and unpack my stuff. My sleeping bag is still damp from the washing line and when **JOSH** sees my camping gear he thinks I've robbed a tramp. I explain about Dad and his money-saving ways and he seems to understand. We've just got everything nice and cosy when the gong goes for dinner.

We gather round the campfire and we're all given a burger to cook ourselves. I want to make sure mine is properly cooked so I leave it on the fire for a little too long. When I whip it off it looks like a piece of coal. No amount of ketchup makes it taste better. Luckily for pudding we're toasting marshmallows!

RESULT!

This was surely an opportunity to impress **CLAUDIA**.

Do you dant me do doast your darsh dellow?

It takes three goes but she finally understands and hands it over. While the marshmallow is toasting we're chatting about **X-WING** — or 'Dex Ding' — and we must have got a little carried away because when I next look over her marshmallow and the stick is on fire! I start to panic and wave it about like a pensioner on Bonfire Night. In an instant **LANCE** is at our side.

He takes the flaming marshmallow stick off me and shoves it in my glass of juice. Thanks, **LANCE**.

CLAUDIA flutters her eyelashes at him and says 'My hero!' **LANCE** flashes his teeth at her and she's nearly blinded.

He gives her another marshmallow and I decide to let her toast it herself. This boyfriend thing isn't working for me at all!

After dinner we all head back for an early night. When **JOSH** unzips the tent there's a terrible smell. If anything it's WORSE than the smell of sick this morning. This is like the skunk had an argument with a nappy down a sewer, pooed itself and then DIED. It seems unpacking my rucksack was a really bad idea. It's just allowed the evil smell to fill the tent! **JOSH** starts to cough and splutter and soon **LANCE** comes over to see what's going on. When he sniffs the stench his smile falters for the first time all day — chalk one up to Fin Spencer! He says it would be 'inhumane' to allow us to sleep in there and insists we sleep in the log cabin again for tonight. Unfortunately it means **JOSH** and I are losing more points from the leaderboard for being 'bad campers'.

Dad comes to help us carry the stuff we need and I tell him to go away. But it's too late. As we're making our way inside **BRAD** sticks his head out from his pop-up tent and waves:

Is the little soldier scared of the dark? Make sure your daddy gives you a goodnight kiss!

He makes **kissy kissy** noises and laughs.

Luckily I managed to sneak my diary out of the tent with my bedding so I could change a few things. I can't change the sick bag in the rucksack because that happened yesterday. But I can stop **LANCE** from attacking my nose. If I'd got up early and used my phone to learn the salute then I wouldn't have spent the rest of the day sounding like a duck. Also, diary, I cooked **CLAUDIA** the perfect marshmallow and she called <u>ME</u> her hero tonight instead of **LANCE**.

Come on, diary!

You've got some making up to do.

SUNDAY

Normally on Sundays I'm not up before 10 a.m. and then I spend a good two hours playing **DEATH SQUADRON APOCALYPSE** in my pants. But apparently that's not how it's done at Action Camp. **LANCE** rings the gong at 6.30 a.m. and everybody has to get ready for breakfast. **Even Dad's not happy.**

The shower block is colder than ever so I give myself a quick spray. It's too cold to wash my hair properly and when I get it dry I look like **a punk rock hedgehog.** I splurge on a tonne of gel and slap on my baseball cap.

As I'm heading back to the log cabin I pass **CLAUDIA** and her friends. She smiles and thanks me for the marshmallow. Apparently it was delicious. I grin and say thank you back, and, do you know what, it actually sounds like 'thank you'. Not 'Dank You' or 'Dank Do' or

anything else. **The diary has worked!**
That must mean I know the **Stevie**
Knuckles Salute too. I try it out and
CLAUDIA and her friends watch as I wave
my arms about like **a ninja in a ballet**
lesson. When I'm finished they all just stand
and stare. I know how they feel. Seeing an

Action Hero do his stuff can really take your breath away!

Before breakfast **JOSH** and I take all my stuff out of the tent and pile it on the grass. **JOSH** opens the tent flaps as wide as they go. If we leave it like that all day then by tonight it should be fine. It certainly couldn't be any worse. Who knows, my sleeping bag might actually finally dry!

At breakfast **BRAD** asks if I survived a night in my daddy's room. I ignore him. To be honest some of the sounds Dad was making were scarier than anything you'd hear in a horror movie. His snores sound like a dinosaur attack.

After breakfast **LANCE** announces that we're going to be spending the day

rock-climbing. I start to get excited —
THIS is what I was hoping for!
I think I'm more of a rock-climbing action
hero than a tent-pitching action hero and this
is my chance to get on the leaderboard.

LANCE loads us all up with safety gear
and a packed lunch and we set off into the
woods. After about half an hour we come to
a rock face. **It's huge.** It's so tall I think
I can see a yeti waving at us from the top.
We can't be climbing that . . . **can we?**

Turns out we can. In fact, apparently this
is only the beginner's rock. *The beginner's*
rock! What does the expert's rock look
like? MOUNT KILIMANJARO?

LANCE lays all the safety gear out on
the ground and shows us the ropes. Literally.

What is it with **LANCE** and his ropes? He's got ropes for his tents, ropes for his climbing, he's probably got ropes for his ropes. Next he gets us all to try on a helmet and I have to take off my baseball cap. This is harder than it sounds. It turns out I put so much gel on this morning that <u>my cap is stuck to my head</u>. **JOSH** gives it a yank and it comes away taking some of my hair with it. Thanks, **JOSH**! Now I've got a bald spot and the hair that's left has frozen into spikes!

LANCE tries to wedge a regular helmet over my spikes but it won't fit. In the end he gets the biggest helmet he's got and manoeuvres it so that my hair is sticking out through the holes in the top. I look like a rubbish Viking.

LANCE goes first and shows us where all the hand and foot holes are. He scuttles up like a cross between Spider-Man and a lizard. He waves to us from the top and all the girls are really impressed. He makes it look so easy and I can't wait to have a go. Unfortunately we have to go alphabetically by surname and I'm right at the end. Luckily it gives me time to watch everybody else and spot where all the good hand holes are.

It's nearly lunchtime when I start to climb — or 'make my ascent' as we **Action Heroes** say — and Dad and Mrs Johnson arrive just as I'm about to set off. At first it all goes very well and I'm climbing like a pro. Then things start to go wrong. I've been sitting in the sun so long that my frozen hair gel has started to melt. Before I know it my huge helmet is slipping down over my eyes. **I CAN'T SEE!** I try to push the helmet back, but this means taking one hand off the rock and I end up losing my grip. As I fall I scream so loudly I'm pretty sure they heard me on Saturn.

Luckily the ropes pull tight before I've gone too far and I'm left dangling off the cliff face like a broken yo-yo. **It's terrifying!** Unfortunately I'm the only one who seems to think so. **BRAD RADLEY** thinks it's hysterical! **JOSH, CLAUDIA** and the others are filming it on their camera phones. **Thanks!** Eventually **LANCE** comes to the rescue and ends up giving me a piggyback to the top. **Brilliant!** That's no points for rock-climbing then.

At the top we break out our packed lunches. As I'm munching on a sandwich I try to laugh off what just happened. I smile at **LANCE** and say, 'Thanks, bud! We **Action Heroes** have got to stick together, right?' Then I launch into the **Stevie Knuckles Salute**

and get so carried away I chuck my sandwich off the cliff. Maybe THAT'S why Stevie's always eating bugs . . .

After lunch LANCE announces that we're going to bungee-jump back down to the ground. He leads us to the other side of the cliff where there's this tatty old rope bridge. LANCE decides to do things in reverse order this time so I am going first. Perfect. He attaches a big piece of elastic to my bum and tells me to jump. I look down. The ground is very far away. I feel really dizzy, but my whole class is watching so I can't back down — besides I need the points. I close my eyes, count to three and JUMP

I scream again. (Seriously, those guys on Saturn are thinking about calling the council!)

The fall seems to be going on forever. The ground is rushing towards me. Then I have a thought, what if **LANCE** is trying to kill me? He could see me as a bit of a threat. Maybe he's rigged the jump so that I turn into a Fin pancake! Just when I'm sure I'm about to smash into a rock the elastic pings tight and I fly back up again. Then down again. Up and down, up and down! It's like being on the worst rollercoaster in the world. I end up dangling from the bridge like a rubbish puppet. By the time I'm lowered to the ground my legs are jelly and I've come to the conclusion that I'm not a bungee-jumping kind of Action Hero either.

When we get back to camp I find out why Dad and Mrs Johnson were so late to

114

the rock-climbing. They've given everything I own a good wash. Which is nice of them. What's not so nice of them is that they've hung it all out to dry for everyone to see. Including the emergency Postman Pat pants I got for my birthday! I hadn't noticed before but they've got a hole in the bum right where Postman Pat's body should be. **How's that possible?** Then I remember **ELLIE**'s collage of me. So that's where she got Mr Pat's body from! **BRAD** points at the hole and says,

Look! Fin's trumps are so powerful they melt pants!

Everybody laughs and I gather it all up before things get any worse.

After dinner **LANCE** announces a special treat — a CREATURE FEATURE! The camp has some animals to stroke and hold — if we dare . . .

All the creatures are hidden in tanks and **LANCE** asks for a brave volunteer to go first. I need to make up some points from the disastrous bungee-jumping rock-climbing nonsense, so I put up my hand.

The animals are in tanks covered by cloths on the stage. I make my way up the steps and start to whip off the cloths one by one. The first few animals are fine. There's a tarantula, a lizard and a bat. This is easy. Everybody's really impressed by my bravery and soon they're all up and handling the animals too. It's only when I get to the last tank that things go wrong. I whip off the cloth and when I see what's inside, I want a portal to open up and suck me to another dimension.

There was a **PYTHON** staring back at me.

LANCE got it out and tried to drape it around my neck. I screamed and the bat **BRAD** was holding went beserk! **LANCE** tried to get the python back in the tank, but it was too late. The bat had started to swoop about the place and, in a panic, **JOSH** dropped the tarantula he was holding. When **LANCE** finally got the python back into the tank we all spent the next half-hour looking for the escaped creatures. We found everything EXCEPT THE TARANTULA. Apparently this is my fault! I don't see how! **LANCE** tried to kill me with a python and **JOSH** was the one who dropped the tarantula.

LANCE pops on a film while he heads off to continue the search.

Turns out the film he's picked is

The only good thing is that this time it's NOT in 3D. I sit at the back and hope no one notices me closing my eyes through the scary bits.

As the credits start **CLAUDIA** giggles and says, 'It'll be nice to see how this one finishes.' When her best friend Lisa asks what she means, she explains about our disastrous cinema date. She laughs and says,

Halfway through Fin threw popcorn and lemonade all over me!

I can't believe my ears! I mean **technically** that is what happened, but she made it sound really bad. Anyway, she threw her own lemonade over herself, I only threw the popcorn. As I'm explaining this to everyone and trying to turn it into a bit of a joke, **CLAUDIA** starts to cry. Apparently I ruined her favourite dress — how could I joke about it like that? I'm about to explain that she was the one who brought it up, when she runs from the room in floods of tears. Oh dear.

I spend the next ninety minutes feeling very uncomfortable and trying to avoid shrieking like a witch in a Jacuzzi.

I can't get back to the tent soon enough. **Diary, you need to fix this.**

I DIDN'T SCREAM when I went rock-climbing, bungee-jumping or when I held the python. In fact, I managed to bungee-jump like a professional and had a photo taken of me with the python around my neck. Also — and this is the biggie — I didn't laugh at **CLAUDIA** when she told the cinema story. This boyfriend/girlfriend thing is finally going my way! I should have manned up and taken responsibility. As **Stevie Knuckles** is always saying, sometimes being an **Action Hero** is admitting when you're wrong. If it wasn't **Stevie** saying it, it'd make me want to puke. Anyway, I've already done that once this trip and broken a toilet, so maybe not!

MONDAY

This morning, when I wake up, I run straight to the leaderboard to see if the diary has worked — **and it has!** I've got a load of points! If it hadn't been for the tent disaster I'd be leading already! I knew I had this **Action Hero** stuff nailed (with a little help from my diary, I suppose.) I'm so excited I do a little dance. **CLAUDIA** sees me and giggles. Maybe I should have got out of my pyjama's first! Well, you can't have everything. I'm so pleased about being on the leaderboard and back in **CLAUDIA**'s good books that I take a photo with my camera. Back in the tent **JOSH** keeps telling me how good I was at rock-climbing and bungee-jumping. He never knew I had it in me! Typical – my own best friend doesn't know he's been mates with an **Action Hero** all his life!

I grabbed my wash bag and headed for the shower block. I knew it was going to be cold, but if I'm tough enough to bungee jump I'm tough enough to shower. Besides, if I don't do something about my hair pretty soon birds will be nesting in it!! The shower is colder than a polar bear's fridge, but I brave it. I splurge on some

Magnolia Marvel and rub it in. If I'm honest, the smell is starting to grow on me! I force my hair down onto my head and shiver my way through the shower. When I get out my teeth are chattering like two grannies on a bus, but it's worth it. For the first time since I've arrived my hair is not a total embarrassment!

As I'm heading for breakfast I spot a poster on the camp noticeboard. I head over to have a look. It's a picture of me with a python draped around my neck — result! But unfortunately I don't look as cool as I'd hoped. It looks like the python is strangling me and I seem terrified. Obviously someone — **BRAD RADLEY** — snapped a photo and turned it into a poster.

Underneath he's written

FIN SPENCER – Snake Charmer!
Available for birthdays, weddings and parties.

I tear down the poster and I'm about to throw it in the bin when I think again. At least I draped a python round my shoulders (even if I didn't, if you know what I mean). I'm going to keep the poster as a souvenir.

I make my way into the dining room and queue up for breakfast. **LANCE** spots me and comes over. He flashes me a smile so bright it burns my retinas, and congratulates me on facing my fears the day before. I smile back. I feel more like an **Action Hero** every

minute – <u>this is easy!</u>

As I'm munching through my scrambled eggs, **CLAUDIA** comes to sit next to me. Apparently I was so nice about the cinema story yesterday that to say thank you she's got me some <u>more</u> Choco Chews. Seriously, where is she getting them from? We're in the middle of NOWHERE. She must have a Choco Chew mine under her tent! I unwrap it as she watches me and I'm about to have to pop it in my mouth when Mrs Johnson comes over – RESULT! Thank you, Mrs Johnson. She's got something for me. She found it while she was cleaning out my rucksack. It's the collage **ELLIE** did of me that was stuck to the fridge. **ELLIE** must have sneaked it into my rucksack when I wasn't looking! **BRAD RADLEY** sees and starts to laugh. **CLAUDIA** compliments me on my eyes, all seven of them! This is a

Everyone thinks I've brought my sister's collage to Action Camp. How 'Action Hero' is that?! To make matters worse, **ELLIE**'s written a little poem on the back about how much she's going to miss me. Before I can stop her Mrs Johnson is reading it out loud.

**My brother Fin
is very smart,
He helps me when
I do my art,**

I'm going to miss him
lots and lots,
He's the bestest brother
I've got.

I'm the <u>only</u> brother she's got, but that's not the point. Dad thinks it's cute, of course. I think it's the most hideous thing I've ever heard. When I get home I'm going to kill my sister, if being an **Action Hero** doesn't kill me first . . .

After breakfast **LANCE** fills us in on the plan for the day. Apparently we're going pot-holing. I have no idea what that is, but it sounds like something to do with snooker. It sounds like fun.

I couldn't have been more **WRONG.**

Pot-holing has nothing to do with snooker. It involves more crash helmets, and — **surprise surprise!** — lots of ropes. Basically, you jump down a tiny hole into a cave and crawl about in it for hours like some kind of human mole until you come out the other side. Who thinks these things up? <u>Seriously!</u> Why can't **Action Heroes** just spend a day sitting by a swimming pool having their feet massaged or something?

LANCE leads us out into the woods and up into the mountains. After about an hour we reach a cave. Apparently that's where we're going to start pot-holing from. **LANCE** ropes us all together, pops helmets on our heads and turns on his torch. He's going first and we're all going to follow behind like some kind of **kiddie** conga.

What follows is the <u>WORST THREE</u> <u>HOURS OF MY LIFE</u>. We all shuffle into the dark and start to ooh and aah at stalagmites or stalagtites or whatever they're called. To be honest, if you've seen one stalagmite you've seen them all. Which is just as well, because soon the cave is getting too narrow for stalagmites and we have to crawl on our bellies through the slime and sludge. To make matters worse the whole cave stinks and something keeps dripping on my head.

Just when I think it can't get any worse, it does. I'm about to crawl under a particularly low-hanging rock to get into a cavern on the other side when I dodge to avoid a drip and end up getting wedged like a human slug. The others manage to unhitch from my rope and wriggle past me into the cavern but I'm stuck! I start to panic, what if I'm going to be stuck down here forever!

Luckily **LANCE** has a solution. He has a big pot of grease in his backpack for 'just such an occasion'. What's he talking about? You mean this has happened before and they still bring kids down here? Before I can argue he's wriggled back to me and is smearing grease all over me. Then he grabs hold of my arms and starts to pull. I'm not budging. He asks **JOSH** and **BRAD** to help and soon everyone is pulling. With a loud pop I come free . . .

LEAVING MY TROUSERS BEHIND.

This can't be over soon enough.

Luckily we don't have much further to go and soon we're crawling up from the cavern and into daylight. What has **LANCE** done? I'm half naked and covered in more grease than a car axel. **It's everywhere!** The stuff stinks and it's bright green. I look like I'm starring in a film.

Everyone else is heading off for more pot-holing but **LANCE** thinks it would be a good idea if I went back to camp for a shower. I think it would be a good idea if I went back to camp and burned it to the ground so other kids don't have to go through this! I don't say anything, I just nod — accidentally on purpose splattering **BRAD RADLEY** with goo — and head home.

I'm so grossed out by the grease that I don't even notice how cold the shower is and when I'm finished I've used half a bottle of Magnolia Marvel. I've never been cleaner, or smelled more like an old lady's perfume cabinet.

When Dad gets back from pot-holing we have a video call with Mum and **ELLIE**.

They've arrived in **PRINCESS TWINKLE'S MAGIC FAIRY LAND** and they show us their bedroom. **It's pinker than a piglet's bottom. ELLIE** loves it and to be honest I'm a little bit jealous. There's a comfy bed, a widescreen TV and a shower with hot water! **They've got it all.** Even I'd risk dancing with a spoon called Nigel to have those luxuries on hand right now.

After dinner **LANCE** lights up the campfire again and we all sit around it while he tells us a spooky story. It's really good, and utterly terrifying. It's all about this mad axe-murderer who hides in the trees and waits for children to walk past. When the murderer sees a kid he jumps out of the tree, waves the axe above his head and yells,

Who's for the chop?

Afterwards I can tell that everyone is on edge.

When **LANCE** is finished the boys decide on a game of football but **CLAUDIA** comes over and asks if I want to go for a walk around the campsite instead. I can't believe my ears — so long as she doesn't bring any Choco Chews with her I'm in! It's what I've been dreaming about ever since I found out we were coming to Stevie Knuckles' Action Adventure Camp! I tell the boys I'm going for a walk with **CLAUDIA** and we head off.

Unfortunately **BRAD RADLEY** must have decided that football wasn't for him either because when we're about halfway through the woods he leaps out of a tree waving a branch above his head and yelling 'Who's for the chop?!' I'm so scared I push **CLAUDIA** to one side and run for it. I'm nearly back to camp before I realise what's happened. **BRAD RADLEY** is laughing like a hyena at a comedy club and **CLAUDIA** is looking at me like I've just stamped on a butterfly. She's really annoyed because if **BRAD** had been a mad axe-murderer I'd have saved myself and left her to die. She wants to know what kind of Action Hero I am anyway?

I try to convince her that I knew it was

BRAD all along, and obviously if there had been a <u>real</u> axe-murderer I'd have shown him my kung fu skills, or at least tried to scare him off with the **Stevie Knuckles Salute**. She isn't having any of it, though, and apparently our walk is over.

I head back to the tent and zip myself in. **Today has been rubbish.** I may have started near the top of the leaderboard but it's been downhill ever since. I know I shouldn't rely on the diary to fix everything, but being a twelve-year-old **Action Hero** is hard!

Dear diary, today, I <u>didn't</u> get stuck down a pot hole, I just let the drip drip on me, OK?

And I <u>didn't</u> run away when **BRAD** jumped out of the tree. In fact, I stood my ground, yelled 'Come and get it!' and saved the day.

Are you listening, diary?

Make this happen for me and tomorrow I'll try and make sure I don't have to use you at all. I'll be the **Action Hero** I know I am inside.

TUESDAY

When I get into the breakfast room this morning I find a **very angry BRAD RADLEY** waiting for me. He's **angry** because I'm top of the leaderboard — result! He's also **angry** because I bopped him on the nose while saving **CLAUDIA** from a mad axe-murderer — double result! The best bit is I'm not in trouble for any of this — triple result! Everyone seems to agree that **BRAD** was playing a mean trick and I did the one thing any **Action Hero** would do in those circumstances.

I can't believe my luck. Top of the leaderboard and **CLAUDIA**'s hero — yesterday was clearly a very good day, even if the diary means I don't remember any of it. I sit down between **CLAUDIA** and **JOSH** and tuck into a bacon sandwich. While I'm munching away people come over to congratulate me and ask me to tell the story of what happened last night. The only problem is I don't know what happened last night. So I start to make it up. . .

In the fifth retelling I'm practically swinging on a vine like Tarzan and better at kung fu than Bruce Lee.

JOSH starts to laugh. He says it was good but not that good. I tell him he's just jealous because he's the second best **Action Hero** in our tent. This makes **JOSH** really angry and he says at least he's got a tent, which is a fair point. He storms off in a huff but I have a captive audience, so I tell the story for the sixth time — this time I'm wearing shades and a bandana.

When I get back to the tent I find that Josh has emptied out all my stuff. Now he's the best **Action Hero** in the tent and I'm the best **Action Hero** OUT of it! I can't believe **JOSH** is being so <u>childish</u>. I try to find my old tent, but **LANCE** presumed it was rubbish and has dumped it in the big bin by the log cabin. Now it's covered

in rubbish and smells of days' old burger sick.
This is a

I think about making some sort of hovel out of sticks — but who am I kidding? So I do the only thing I can do. I gather up all my stuff and move back into Dad's room. It should be fine so long as I don't talk to him, I am top of the leaderboard after all.

We spend the rest of the morning learning how to find our own food in an emergency. This doesn't mean ordering an online delivery, though — apparently it means knowing which berries and plants are good to eat and learning how to fish.

LANCE takes us out to the lake on the edge of the camp and teaches us to fish. Along the way he tells us about foraging and points out the good berries and the bad berries. How is anyone supposed to know the difference? They're both red! Then we spend the rest of the morning down by the lake with a fishing rod each.

I've never caught a fish in my life. As far as I'm concerned, if you want to find a fish you either go to the fish shop or the pet shop. However, that's not how **LANCE** wants us to do it. He breaks out a bucket of maggots and a load of fishing rods and tells us to

get busy.

The maggots look like little **zombie bogies** and no one wants to touch them but **BRAD** digs his hand in and sticks one on his fishing hook. I don't want to be outdone by **BRAD** so I dig my hand in too. The maggots feel **disgusting**. It's like your hand is being tickled to death by slugs.

I stick one onto my fishing hook, march purposefully towards the edge of the water, tell everyone to stand well back and prepare to cast off. Just as I'm pulling my arms back **BRAD** flicks a maggot down the back of my t-shirt. I jump so high the fishing line ends up in the tree. **BRAD** laughs. **LANCE** didn't see what happened and says,

You won't find many fish up there, Fin!

No kidding. I spend the next half an hour trying to untangle my fishing line while a greedy bird eats the maggot.

When I finally get it free I sacrifice another zombie bogie and dangle the line in the water. I don't see what's particularly 'action-y' about fishing. It takes AGES. You just sit there in the peace and quiet waiting for **NOTHING TO HAPPEN!**

Eventually though, I get a bite — this is more like it. The fish on the end of my line must be a beast — it's like playing tug-o-war with a tractor! Now I can see what all the fuss is about. It's man versus fish and we're fighting to the bitter end!

Soon I'm sweating like a rhino on a treadmill and I'm convinced I've hooked some kind of mutant shark-piranha. I call for help and **LANCE** appears at my side: we're the centre of attention. I've really got a <u>whopper</u> on the end of the line; they'll probably take a photo for the paper. I can practically smell the trophy. **LANCE** and I give it one big tug and when I see what comes out of the water I can't believe my eyes.

Fincredible Fin Spencer, Action Hero, has managed to catch . . .

a shopping trolley.

I'm a laughing stock and decide to hang up my fishing rod for good. If I'm starving to death and the only thing to do is fish, I'll just have to die! (Unless I was lucky enough to catch a trolley full of food, I guess.) I decide to stick to foraging for berries and head to one of the two bushes **LANCE** showed us earlier. Just as I'm about to tuck into my haul, Dad arrives and gobbles the lot. Before I know what's happening he's eaten half a bush full! I knew I was ignoring him for a reason!

I'm starving, but there's no time for that because **LANCE** announces that we're staying by the lake for a team-building exercise. He goes to a shed and comes out with a load of wood, some barrels and — yup, you've guessed it — more ropes!

I swear if I see another rope I'm going to lasso a jumbo jet and get the hell out of here!

He splits us into teams and tells us all to build a raft using the stuff he's laid out on the shore. Unfortunately **LANCE** puts **JOSH**, **BRAD** and me in a team together. If ever there was a team that didn't work it was this one! **BRAD** isn't talking to me because of the whole axe- murderer nose-bop thing, I'm not talking to **BRAD** because of the maggot thing and **JOSH** isn't talking to me because of the whole breakfast thing.

We just stare at each other for half an hour, then, when it's obvious no one is going to do anything I take charge and lay out some planks of wood. I wrap them in rope and try to tie a knot. The other teams are way ahead. **CLAUDIA** and her friends are already paddling into the centre of the lake! I tell the other two to co-operate or we'll be at the bottom of the leaderboard. This does the trick and soon our raft is finished. I think. It's hard to tell, because basically it looks like a rubbish garden fence. We set sail anyway. **BRAD** and **JOSH** paddle while I bark orders. They start grumbling, which is hardly fair. I did all the hard work, the least they can do is paddle the thing!

At first it's all going well and it looks like we might just catch up with the others. I shout at them to go faster and **BRAD** has a strop. He throws down the paddle and tells me that no one tells him what to do. As he's shouting his paddle falls overboard and now we're going in circles! **JOSH** says if **BRAD**'s not paddling then neither is he and he throws his paddle overboard too. I am surrounded by morons! We wave for help and **LANCE** comes to rescue us in a dinghy just as HMS Useless sinks beneath the waves. It looks like no points for us today!

The only thing that cheers me up is dinner.

It's delicious, and for once it's not cooked on a campfire. We all tuck into some beans and sausages, apart from Dad who's got a bit of a tummy ache. Apparently I'd foraged the wrong berries and they were playing havoc with his insides. Serves him right for being so greedy!

After dinner we all gather around the campfire for a sing-song. **LANCE** has a guitar and he starts off by singing my favourite *X-WING* song. It turns out he's got a really good voice and he's singing the song I was going to sing. How unfair is that!? **JOSH** goes next and he sings a System of the Future song that I wrote. It's all about **CLAUDIA** but she doesn't know that.

You make my knees go weak
You make it hard to speak
I love your smile
and I love your curls,
You're my number one girl.

Everyone thinks **JOSH** is BRILLIANT. It's not fair — that's my song. But when I say as much **LANCE** tells me not to be so mean-spirited, which I'm pretty sure is **LANCE**-speak for 'sulky'. I'm not being mean-spirited or mean-anything, it's just that it's my song. I wrote it about **CLAUDIA**! The campfire goes quiet and I realise I was so angry I said that last bit OUT LOUD. **BRAD** starts to snigger and my cheeks go bright red.

To try to save the situation Dad fights through the pain, takes the guitar and starts to sing an old song he knows from the Stone Age or something — who knew they even had guitars back then? It's so embarrassing I want to throw myself on the campfire. But it seems that I'm the only one who thinks that. When Dad's finished he gets a round of applause. What's wrong with these people? Have their ears gone on holiday to Honalulu or something?

I grab the guitar to show them how it's done and launch into a particularly angry **X-WING** song called 'Pig Splat'. It goes on for twenty minutes. Just as I'm getting into my third guitar solo **LANCE** decides it's time for bed. I knew he wasn't a **TRUE X-WING** fan like me!

I head over to Dad's cabin and settle down for a good night's sleep. Which is easier said than done. The berries Dad ate are doing funny things to his tummy and he's trumping louder than an elephant brass band. The noise is bad enough, but the smell is worse. There's **NO WAY** I can get to sleep.

I break out the diary and try to think of a way to fix things. This morning was brilliant but I could have done without catching a shopping trolley and sinking a raft. If I got up early yesterday and researched top fishing techniques and the basics of raft-building on the camp computer then I'd have aced it. **COME ON, DIARY**, you're doing so well, don't fail this **Action Hero** now! Tomorrow I'll go it alone — promise!

WEDNESDAY

Last night I had the worst night's sleep EVER. Every time I was just drifting off to sleep Dad would let rip with another toxic trump that sounded like a sonic boom. When **LANCE** rang the gong this morning our room smelled like an explosion at a stink-bomb factory.

The only thing that made getting up worthwhile was the leaderboard. My name was right at the top. I was in joint first place with **BRAD RADLEY** – result!

At breakfast **LANCE** told me that he'd **NEVER** seen anyone build a raft that fast. It turns out I was a bit of whitewater hero, too, because when some of the other rafts started sinking I paddled to the rescue. It's all in a day's work for a real life **Action Hero**.

The diary worked! Had I caught any fish? I found out soon enough. When I got outside **BRAD** had mocked up another poster of me for all to see. I was standing surrounded by a load of fish, holding an eel above my head. **BRAD** had put a speech bubble coming out of my mouth.

It said,

My name is Fin and I've got fishy fingers!

Laugh it up, **BRAD** – you're just jealous.

After breakfast **LANCE** divided us into two teams and told us to get ready for today's adventure. This morning we were orienteering, which it turns out is a posh way of saying

treasure hunt,

or, in my case,

getting lost.

We had to use a map to find five things hidden in the woods. The losing team would have to cook dinner for the winning team. As **BRAD** and I were at the top of the leaderboard he made us team captains. There was **NO WAY** I was losing this one.

Turns out, I was WRONG. I've never been

ANY good at map reading — I mean, what is the point? Grown-ups always know where to go and if that fails there's the maps app on my phone. Just as I was thinking about taking out my phone for a crafty bit of cheating **LANCE** confiscated them all! Spoilsport.

LANCE showed us how to check for broken twigs and look for footprints, and then he sent both teams off into the woods armed with nothing more than a map, a compass and a list of **weird** things to find. I mean, who needs **a heart-shaped stone** and a **blue sock**? It was like **a madman's shopping list**. Everyone looked to me, and because as far as they were concerned, I had been aceing all the **Action Hero** stuff,

I had to take charge. It was time to step up.

At first it was fine, there was a path to follow and I had a blue sock with me that I dropped 'accidentally on purpose' so we could find it. But then the path disappeared and we were soon very lost. We hadn't found anything on the list since the blue sock and then **CLAUDIA**, who was on my team, pointed out that I was holding the map upside-down.

We headed back in the opposite direction but I managed to lead us into some sort of swamp. I got stuck in the mud and it took three people to pull me out again. Unfortunately both of my shoes came off and disappeared in some yucky brown bubbles.

Well, real **Action Heroes** don't need shoes anyway!

Once I was out of the swamp I pushed through some trees on the hunt for the **heart-shaped stone**. Unfortunately I was so keen to get going that I let go of the branch a little too fast and thwacked **CLAUDIA** in the face. **Oops!** She started to cry and her eye started to swell. Just when things couldn't get any worse I lost the compass and it started to rain. We spent twenty minutes in a cave waiting for it to pass. **It didn't**. My team were starting to think about mutiny so I decided we needed to abandon the list and get back to camp fast.

Unfortunately without the compass I had

162

no idea where we were going. Then I remembered that the Swiss Army knife had a compass on it somewhere. I fiddled with it for five minutes but the only thing that popped out was that annoying little hook. I think it must be broken or something. **What is that hook for anyway?**

1. Eyebrow straightener
2. Portable coat rack for mice
3. Catching tadpoles

After about an hour we found **LANCE**. We'd been gone so long that he'd come looking for us. When we got back to camp my team looked like they'd just survived a natural disaster. We still had only the one blue sock and both my shoes were missing. To make matters worse **BRAD** and his team had collected everything. It looked like we were cooking dinner this evening.

Before that, though, **LANCE** had one more 'bit of fun' for us, which we all know is **LANCE**-speak for 'torture'. Around the back of the camp there is an assault course. It's made of wood and rope — of course — and quite frankly looks like the sort of thing even the army would think twice about using because it looked so dangerous. **LANCE** thought it would be a good idea for us to be 'put through our paces', which we all know is **LANCE**-speak for killed! Can't he see it's still raining?

We all traipse out and **LANCE** gets out

his stopwatch. The assault course is **TERRIFYING**. There are balance beams, huge tractor tyres, massive walls, a scramble net and a death slide. That's right, a **DEATH** slide – the clue's in the name, people! Anyway, I seem to be the only person who thinks this is a really bad idea. We all line up at the start and just when I think this can't get any more dangerous **LANCE** gets out a **GUN! Has he gone mad?** It turns out it's only a starting pistol, but how was I supposed to know?

As I climb back out from behind the bush I'd dived into, **LANCE** fires the pistol for us to begin. Together the class squelches and splats it's way around the obstacles. It's like the worst PE lesson ever. By the time

165

we get to the first object — some tyres you have to hop in and out of — I already feel more exhausted than **a granny on a trampoline**. I hop in and out of the tyres and then try to clamber over the wall. **JOSH** gives me a helpful push and I topple head first over the top and splat into a muddy puddle. Thanks, **JOSH**. After I get my head stuck in the scramble net I decide to abandon the balance beam altogether. When I reach the death slide I'm starting to hope that the name is genuine and I'm about to plummet to my doom. Eventually the horror is over. I'm soaking wet and grateful not to be in last place. That prize goes to **CLAUDIA**. To be honest she's finding it a bit tricky to see through her swollen eye.

Today had been the worst day ever, but it wasn't over yet. While **BRAD** and his team sat in the dining room like a medieval royal family, my team had to wait on them hand and foot. We cooked burgers, poured juice and even did the washing-up! By nine o'clock I was ready for bed. Just as we were putting away the pots and pans, **CLAUDIA** came over. Her eye was looking very sore, but she was still smiling. She said she had something to cheer me up and produced a bumper bag of Choco Chews.

Nooooooo!

It was the final straw. Maybe it was because I'm more tired than a mammoth in a marathon, or because I've just cooked **BRAD RADLEY** dinner, or because I lost my shoes, or because I have a broken Swiss Army knife but I snapped!

I tell **CLAUDIA** that I don't like Choco Chews, I've never liked Choco Chews and I don't want to eat any more Choco Chews. In fact, they taste like a rancid sponge!

CLAUDIA's bottom lip begins to wobble. Apparently she's bought them for me <u>specially</u> and now she feels really stupid.

She wants to know why I didn't tell her I didn't like Choco Chews when she first offered me one. I tell her that I didn't want to hurt her feelings. But she says her feelings are more hurt than ever now. **CLAUDIA** rushes from the dinner hall and I end the day shoeless, clueless and Choco Chew-less.

Diary, you need to fix this. I can do something about the orienteering. If I'd given **CLAUDIA** the map and compass then we'd have been all right. She'd have been in front so wouldn't have got thwacked with a tree branch. She's also **brilliant** at geography so we wouldn't have got lost. Who knows, she might even have led us to victory!

The other thing I shouldn't have done is

snap at **CLAUDIA**. She was only trying to be nice and that's something I've wanted for so long. How bad would it be to eat a bumper bag of Choco Chews for the girl you love? Not that bad! So, diary, I ate those Choco Chews and I loved them. Do you hear me? I loved them. I also gave her a big bag of ready-salted crisps I've been saving for an emergency. Now if you'll excuse me I'm so tired I need to . . .

Zzzz

Zzz

Zz . . .

Z . . .

z . . .

z . . .

z . . .

z . . .

z . . .

THURSDAY

This morning Dad woke me up by stepping ON MY HEAD. Seriously. Apparently he forgot I was there! Thanks, Dad. I need to get my own space. After another freezing Magnolia Marvel shower I decide I need to try and get my tent back up before tonight. Even if it's covered in stinky stains and draughtier than a pair of clown's trousers it's better than spending another night with Dad.

I decide to cheer myself up by checking out the leaderboard. **CLAUDIA** is right at the top next to **BRAD**. Apparently she did such a good job with the compass and map yesterday the rest of my team voted her new leader and **LANCE** gave her all the points. Way to go, diary! But that's not all. She's not speaking to me because she thinks I'm GREEDY. Apparently she broke out the Choco Chews last night and I ate every single one when she wanted to share. I ate so many I had to rush to the loo and stayed in there for an hour and a half. Thanks, diary! That's NOT what I had in mind.

This is a

Even with a magic diary I'm not the **Action Hero** or boyfriend I know I should be.

After breakfast I take **JOSH** to one side and persuade him to help me put my tent up this afternoon. At first he's not interested. He's still angry over the argument we had. **What a baby!** Then I remember I've got a chocolate bar in my bag and I bribe him with the promise of a midnight feast. He says yes **quicker than a lottery winner in a car showroom.** I knew the fastest way to **JOSH**'s heart was through his stomach . . .

Before that, though, **LANCE** wants to teach us some survival skills. To be honest I've been doing pretty well for the first twelve years of my life, but apparently that isn't the point. He wants to make sure that if we're ever dropped into a jungle we'll know how to get out alive. What does he know that I don't? Do Mum and Dad have some plans for my next summer holiday or something?

LANCE takes us into the woods and tells us to make a shelter. I get the biggest leaf I can find and hold it over my head like an umbrella.

Apparently that wasn't what he had in mind.

He wants us to weave branches and sticks together and make a little hut. This is ridiculous.

Dad is really keen to help. He says the sooner I can build my own house the sooner I'll move out of his. Not funny, Dad!

BRAD and the others are really getting into it, but I just can't see the point. If ever I'm dropped into a jungle I'll be trying to get out, not building myself a house to live in! I find a tree with some low-hanging branches and try to make them into a roof. I crawl inside and it feels pretty cosy! I'm just thinking about where I'll put the sofa when **LANCE** comes over with a worried look on his face. Apparently I'm sitting on an ant's nest.

I look down and see that **LANCE** is right. Hundreds of ants are crawling all over my legs! I try to wipe them off, but they're everywhere. Then **LANCE** chucks a whole flask of water over me to wash them away. When he's finished, I look like I've wet myself.

Thanks, **LANCE**, you really know how to help a guy out.

Once we've all got our shelters up **LANCE** gives us each two sticks and a tin of beans. He tells us to make a fire to cook the beans on. It sounds like fun. The only problem is my fire won't start! I was hoping the two sticks would be matchsticks, but oh no, that would be too easy! Apparently if you rub twigs together for long enough you get fire.

I'm rubbing and **rubbing** and **rubbing** but the only thing I'm getting is hand ache. It doesn't help that **JOSH** practically has **the Great Fire of London** in front of him. Everyone else seems to be getting it too. Pretty soon the air is full of the smell of bubbling baked beans.

After half an hour I give up on the fire and eat the beans cold. I think that's what a real **Action Hero** would do anyway . . .

Just as I'm finishing off my beans my legs start to itch. They're covered in huge red blobs. I look like I've got monster measles.

LANCE diagnoses an allergy to ant bites and gives me some cream that <u>smells like a bottom</u>. Thanks again, **LANCE**.

When we get back to camp, **JOSH** and I spend an hour putting up my tent. **JOSH** is actually pretty good at this, or at least he is now. It seems like he's actually been learning stuff on this **Action Camp**! Pretty soon we've got the tent up and I've moved all my stuff in. It's nice to finally have a tent of my own to sleep in, and thanks to **LANCE**'s stinky cream my bites have stopped itching.

Before bed Dad and I have another video call with Mum and **ELLIE**. They don't look like they're having quite such a good time anymore. Apparently it hasn't stopped raining for thirty-six hours and PRINCESS TWINKLE'S MAGIC FAIRY LAND has had to close. A bolt of lightning hit the 'The Toaster Coaster' and they had to close 'Nigel's World of Spoons'! Typical — the only exciting thing to ever happen at PRINCESS TWINKLE'S MAGIC FAIRY LAND and they close the place down.

After the video call I head for my tent and invite **JOSH** in for our midnight feast. It's not quite midnight (it's actually only nine thirty) but **JOSH** doesn't seem to mind. He brings over a bag of crisps, but they're already open because he's been nibbling them all week! I dig my hand in anyway and when I pull it out there's a fat tarantula sitting on top. I scream like a

Shih Tzu on a seesaw and flick it onto **JOSH**.
He screams even louder. Soon the whole camp
is awake and crowding around our tent. **JOSH**
and I run out in our pyjamas shouting about
the tarantula. **LANCE** dives in and comes
out with it cupped in his hands. That's how a
real **Action Hero** would do it. Everybody's
laughing at me and **JOSH**, and Mrs Johnson
confiscates our crisps and sweets as

punishment for having an illegal midnight feast
— even though it was only half-past nine!

I go back to my tent and try to get to
sleep but my legs are itchier than a nit with
nits. I decide to break out the diary. Today
would have been so much better if I hadn't
got covered in ant bites.

So, diary, instead of hiding in a bush I
did my best to make a genuine shelter, OK?
No ants! Also, when I found that tarantula in
the crisps I DIDN'T scream, I coolly and calmly
took it back to the tank, Action Hero
style.

FRIDAY

This morning I was woken up by a foghorn, although as far as I was concerned it wasn't morning at all, it was **THE MIDDLE OF THE NIGHT!** It was still dark outside. I could see stars, for goodness' sake! The only things that should be awake at that time are vampire owls. At least my legs were no longer itching

— thank you, diary.

I turned on my torch and checked my watch. It was five a.m. and that noise wasn't getting any quieter. It sounded like an elephant with a head cold. I crawled out of my tent and found **LANCE** grinning like a mad thing, finger pressed down on the aerosol hooter he was holding. Everyone else emerged from their tents like badgers with headaches and finally **LANCE** took his finger off the hooter. We all breathed a sigh of relief but not for long, because next the six-foot tooth factory broke out a MEGAPHONE and started to shout!

Apparently we all had half an hour to get dressed and meet in the Welcome Circle. Before **LANCE** left he congratulated me for finding the tarantula and gave me fifteen bonus points. I should be happy, but did I mention it's FIVE A.M.!?

I don't bother to have a shower, I just spray some deodorant over the top of my clothes and hope no one will notice. By the time we get to the Welcome Circle it's just about getting light, which is a shame because none of us are at our best. We look like the survivors of a plane crash but **LANCE** is still smiling. I think he might be some sort of robot.

He claps his hands together and explains that we're about to start the final phase of our **Action Hero** training, which sounds a bit sinister if you ask me. It turns out it's time for the **Stevie Knuckles' Action Hero Wilderness Weekend**. The Wilderness Weekend is a chance for us to put everything we've learned into practice. I feel a lump in my throat. I've learned *nothing*, apart from the fact that I don't like Choco Chews, but I knew that before I even got here.

Apparently we're going to spend two days out in the wild, living, breathing and eating nature. It's a chance for us to get a few last-minute points to try to win the trophy. **LANCE** tells us to pack everything we need into our rucksacks and meet back in an hour.

I can't believe it — I've **FINALLY** got my tent up and now I'm taking it down again! Life is so unfair. I spend the next hour trying to remember how everything packs down. When I'm finished my backpack looks like an explosion in a laundrette. There's bits spilling out of the top and I have to use my foot to stamp my sleeping bag inside.

I hoist the backpack onto my shoulders. It's so heavy it feels like I'm giving a piggyback to a real pig. The only person smiling is **BRAD RADLEY**. Because his gear is so modern his backpack is lighter than a ballerina's breakfast and he practically jogs out of camp. Before we go **LANCE** makes us hand in all our mobile phones again so we can't cheat. He leaves them with Mrs Johnson, who is staying to 'man base camp', which we all know is teacher-speak for 'read gossip mags'.

LANCE gives **CLAUDIA** a map and shows us the place where we'll be making camp for the night. It's miles away! **LANCE** says it'll take us three hours to get there, so we'd better get cracking. I start to trudge behind **CLAUDIA** and soon we're deep in the woods. The map leads us up a mountain, which is hard going. It feels like I'm going to belch out a lung. When we get to the top we reach a big chasm. I can't see any way of getting across apart from the threadbare rope bridge we bungee-jumped off.

When I step onto the bridge it creaks like a rusty bicycle. It's a long way down. I step from plank to plank and try to keep my eyes on the other side. **BRAD** has gone first, and he's waiting on the other side. He's grinning at me. When I'm halfway across he starts to sway the bridge with his arms. I cling on for dear life and rock back and forth. I've got two choices, stay where I am and wait for the bridge to collapse or keep on walking. I decide to keep on walking. I can't get off that bridge soon enough.

Unfortunately, when I get off the bridge things don't get much better. **CLAUDIA** leads us down a twisty gravel path with a drop to one side. By now my backpack is digging into my shoulders and I'm ready to give up.

The only thing that stops me is that if I gave up there and then I'd be stranded halfway up a mountain. **LANCE** can't understand what's happened to me. I've been such an **Action Hero** all week, why am I complaining so much now? The thing is, I haven't been an **Action Hero** at all — the diary's just been making it look that way.

I want to curl into a ball and pretend I'm a hedgehog. The last thing we have to do on our way to camp is an aerial assault course. Gulp. Basically someone has taken all the worst bits of the assault course we did earlier in the week and PUT THEM UP A TREE. Why would you do that? We have to clamber up to a platform, clip ourselves to a rope and set off through the treetrops.

Just as I'm setting off it starts to get windy. The trees are swaying like little girls at a ᴄʜᴀʀʟɪᴇ ᴅɪᴍᴘʟᴇs concert. I panic and freeze. **CLAUDIA** comes to help, but I'm so scared I end up dragging her off the platform with me. We end up dangling from the safety rope like a couple of Christmas tree decorations.

CLAUDIA giggles and tries to see the funny side, but I can't join in and when **LANCE** eventually comes to the rescue **CLAUDIA** smiles sweetly at him instead. She ends up hanging out with **LANCE** up front and with me bringing up the rear.

When we finally get to the clearing I put up my tent and clamber inside. Dad gets in after me! What's he doing? It turns out that because this is technically his tent we're sharing again. I don't believe my ears! I'd only just got rid of him, and if we're sharing the tent how come I had to carry it the whole way? Dad smiles and says he didn't want to cost me any more points on the leaderboard. He's all heart.

JOSH rustles up a roaring campfire and

soon we're cooking sausages and swapping stories. I should be happy, but I'm not. I've had a rubbish day AGAIN and **CLAUDIA** is all eyes for **LANCE**, not me. I head back into the tent to write in the diary. But when I get inside I stop myself. All of this trouble is coming from me pretending to be someone that I'm not. I said I liked Choco Chews when I don't, I'm trying to be an Action Hero when I'm not cut out for it. Maybe I should stop trying to be all of these things and just be myself. It certainly couldn't go any worse and I might actually enjoy myself.

So tonight, I'm not going to change anything. I flunked the first half of the Wildernesss Weekend and I'm sharing a tent with my dad. That's who Fin Spencer really is.

I'm not an **Action Hero**, I'm an **Action ZERO**.

Maybe it's about time I accepted that.

SATURDAY

Want to know how to go from **Action ZERO** to **Action Hero** in one day? Then buckle up, because I'm about to tell you! Last night I went to bed as the biggest loser on Planet Loser, but tonight . . . Well, we'll get to that.

The day started badly, again. I woke up with a big red mark on my face because apparently I'd pitched my tent on top of a rock and then fallen asleep on it. The only good thing about the beginning of the day was that there was no cold shower, so I couldn't have one, although it was <u>still</u> raining, which was kind of the same thing. For breakfast **LANCE** broke out these energy bars. They were so disgusting I'd rather eat an entire sweet shop's worth of Choco Chews! Honestly, they tasted like a pirate's beard.

And before you say anything, I **DO** know what a pirate's beard tastes like. I went to a fancy dress party dressed as one once and nearly choked on the face fungus.

Anyway, back to this morning. After our disgusting breakfast **LANCE** told everyone to break camp, which is **LANCE**-speak for 'pack up'. Dad didn't want me to lose any points so didn't help me with the tent at all – **thanks, Dad!** When I'd finished I lifted the backpack onto my shoulders and promptly fell backwards. I must have looked like a **stranded turtle.** Dad helped me back onto my feet – useful at last! – and we set off.

By now, everyone had decided after yesterday that all the cool stuff I'd done in the week must have been some kind of fluke.

It was clear I was a complete dweeb when it came to this **Action Hero** stuff.

Because my camping gear was so old, it was heavier than everybody else's and soon I was lagging well behind. **LANCE** kept shouting at me to 'keep up'. Which we all know is **LANCE**-speak for 'Run like a gazelle, loser boy'! By mid morning I was puffing like a puffin in a pedal car. My legs were hurting, my back was hurting, my head was hurting – even my hurts were hurting!

As we marched up another mountain I couldn't keep up any longer. It was time to stop for a rest. I sat down on the path and caught my breath, and watched as my friends made their way up the twisty path ahead and out of sight around a corner.

Just as I was thinking about growing a beard, becoming a hermit and living on the mountain forever, a terrifying noise filled the air. It sounded like an **EARTHQUAKE** or a **VOLCANO** and it was coming from up ahead. I ran to see what had happened. When I got round the corner I couldn't believe my eyes. A mountain of rubble and boulders was blocking the path. I was on one side . . . and **LANCE** and everybody else was on the other!! All the rain must have caused a landslide. The path had fallen away in front of them and to make matters worse they couldn't go round as there was a chasm to one side and a cliff face to the other. They were completely trapped.

LANCE called over the rocks to me.

Apparently I was their only hope.

I had to run back to base camp and get help. I couldn't believe my ears. **LANCE** wanted **ME** to help? The boy who was scared of heights, pythons and cold showers?

Surely there was some kind of mistake! But as I looked through the rocks at **CLAUDIA**, **JOSH**, Dad and the others, I could see **REAL** fear in their eyes. It was time for Fin Spencer to become the **Action Hero** he always knew he was!

I felt a little bit sick.

I left my backpack on the side of the mountain and started to run. I raced back past where we made camp the night before and followed the trail of the treetop assault course from the ground — I knew there was an easier way to do these things! Once I got out of the woods I came to a fork in the path. I wasn't 100% sure which way to go, but then something crazy happened — I started to remember some of the things I'd learned over the past few days. I spot a snapped twig and a muddy footprint and all that tracking nonsense came back to me. Soon I was running back across the rope bridge and heading for home. I even managed to grab a few berries for a snack along the way! The right ones!

Amazing Action Hero skills! What's happened to me?

It was after lunchtime when I got into base camp. Mrs Johnson was there talking to someone with his back turned. When I called for help the stranger turned around and I couldn't believe my eyes. It's **Stevie Knuckles!** The real **Stevie Knuckles,** in the flesh.

He's here to award the **Action Hero trophy** and was waiting for us all to get back. When I explained what had happened he grabbed a rescue rucksack and asked me to show him where the landslide was on the map. He'll go back to rescue everyone.

No way! I'm going with him. This is the chance for me to show this **TV Action Hero** how we do it Fin Spencer style. Mrs Johnson stays to 'man the camp' (which we all know is teacher-speak for 'read even more gossip mags').

Stevie Knuckles and I race back over the rope bridge and soon we're running into the woods side by side. **I can't believe what's happening.** This is what I dreamed about. I'm running side by side to the rescue with **Stevie Knuckles** like a pair of real **Action Heroes**! I show him the footprints and the snapped twigs, I fill him in on what will need to be done when we get there and he tells me he's 'very impressed.' Which we all know is **Stevie**

Knuckles-speak for 'You're my hero, Fin Spencer.'

Just as we get close to where the landslide has happened, **Stevie** makes us stop for something to eat.

It's important we keep our strength up, he says.

I start to get a very bad feeling about this. I tell him there's no way I'm eating any bugs. He can chomp on caterpillars or munch on midges if that's what he likes, but feasting on flies is not for Fin Spencer! He looks at me like I've gone mad and then produces a couple of bananas from his rucksack. Apparently it's not a bug day today.

I lead **Stevie** up the mountain and when **LANCE** and the others see us they breathe a massive sigh of relief. **It's all going to be all right. Stevie** has a shovel strapped to the side of his rucksack and he starts to dig away at the rocks. It's all going very well. **Stevie**'s a hero, **I'm a hero**, and we'll all be home in time for tea.

It's then that it all goes wrong. **Stevie** is so keen to rescue everyone that he's building up a bit of a sweat. He's clearing a little tunnel in the rocks so everyone can crawl out, but just as he's about to take out the final rock, the spade slips out of his hands and **tumbles over the side of the chasm.**

Stevie and I go to have a look. Luckily the spade has a little loop of string on the handle and it's snagged on a branch. **Stevie** tries to reach it, but it's no use — it's just past his fingertips. Then I have a **brilliant** idea. **It's an idea so good it makes my brain hurt!**

I rush to my backpack and take out my Swiss Army knife. I fiddle with it and sure enough **that annoying little hook pops out**. Finally it's going to come in useful! I lie down on my tummy and reach over the edge into the chasm. The drop is so far to the bottom my tummy starts to twirl, but I keep my cool. I use the hook and loop it through the bit of string and carefully pull the shovel back to the path. I hand it to

Stevie, we high five and soon **Stevie** is shovelling away again and <u>I'm a hero</u>. **Again.** So THAT'S what that hook is for — a spade-snagger. Those crazy Swiss, they think of everything!

Soon the tunnel is cleared and **LANCE** and the others are crawling to safety. There's a lot of hugging and back-slapping and everyone agrees that even though Stevie dug the tunnel, it was **FIN SPENCER** who saved the day.

Back at the camp the coach has arrived to take us home, but before we leave there's a small matter of a trophy to award. We all gather round the leaderboard. **BRAD** is right at the top and I am right at the bottom.

It's not looking good.

Then **LANCE** does something BRILLIANT.

He awards me one million points for saving everybody today.

ONE MILLION POINTS!

That puts me at the top of the leaderboard and about nine hundred and ninety thousand, nine hundred and ninety points clear of **BRAD RADLEY**! Everyone gives me a big cheer and **Stevie Knuckles** hands me the trophy, shakes my hand and says,

You can be on my team any time

which we all know is **Stevie Knuckles**-speak for 'Hey kid, let's make a movie together.'

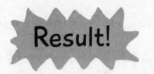

Result!

The only person who isn't happy about any of this is **BRAD RADLEY**, which only makes the trophy shine a little brighter!

We all clamber onto the coach and I get to sit next to **CLAUDIA**. As I'm helping her with her bag, a packet of ready-salted crisps falls out. They're the ones I gave her. Apparently she doesn't really like that flavour, she just said that to make me feel better. We both laugh. I don't like Choco Chews, she doesn't like ready-salted crisps! She says I can have her crisps if she can eat the Choco Chews I've been stuffing in my bag. It's a deal! Maybe we are made for each other after all.

So that's how you go from ZERO to Hero in a day! Pretty cool, huh? And as I sit next to **CLAUDIA**, holding a trophy and heading for home, I wouldn't change a thing.

SUNDAY

The bus finally pulled into school at eight o'clock this morning. I must have drifted off on the coach and when I woke up I had to double-check I still had the trophy. It might all have been a dream. I had nothing to worry about, the trophy was still there and I'm still an **Action Hero**.

Result!

Mum and **ELLIE** are waiting for Dad and I when we hop off the coach. So is **CLIFF**. He's got something for me — the little ball from Cosmic Kick Ball Carnage that's been surgically removed from his nose! I tell him he can keep it for the rematch! **CLIFF** smiles. Bring it on!

I say goodbye to **CLAUDIA** and we agree to go on another date — I'll buy the Choco Chews and she'll buy the crisps!

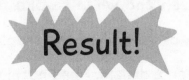

Result!

ELLIE has bought me a pair of fairy wings from PRINCESS TWINKLE'S MAGIC FAIRY LAND. Normally I'd have thrown them in the bin, but I know **ELLIE** must have picked them out especially so I pull them on there and then.

Behind me **BRAD** sniggers. I don't care, **Action Heroes** can wear what they like.

We clamber in the car but instead of driving home **Mum drives us to the airport.**

I'm confused. Where are we going?

It turns out Mum complained about **PRINCESS TWINKLE'S MAGIC FAIRY LAND** being closed and got a load of money back, so she booked us a last-minute holiday to Spain —

RESULT!

She's packed Dad and me a suitcase each and we're all going to spend the last part of the half-term break chilling by the pool.

DOUBLE RESULT!

She thinks we've all had a 'pretty traumatic time', which is Mum-speak for 'nearly died', and it would be good for all of us to spend some time together as a family. For once I agree.

On the plane **ELLIE**'s packed her collage kit and I don't mind helping her. We make a collage of both of us — the **Fincredible Action Hero** and **PRINCESS TWINKLE FAIRY**. It's so good Mum says she's going to frame it and stick it in the toilet when we get home. I think that's a compliment!

When we get to the hotel I get changed into my swimming trunks and go and sit by the pool. Somehow I managed to get a date with **CLAUDIA** and become a real life Action Hero, and what's more I did it all without any help from the diary.

It just goes to show, you don't need to eat bugs or bungee-jump with killer whales to be an Action Hero.

This Fincredible **Action Hero** is scared of snakes, doesn't like heights, is surprisingly good at collages and stinks of *Magnolia Marvel*. He also has the most useless Swiss Army knife ever invented — **way to go, hero!**

I think it's time to say goodbye to this diary again. This **Action Hero** needs to rescue his Mum from an ice cream. And as for the **Stevie Knuckles Salute** — well, it looks even better when you're wearing a pair of fairy wings!

Instructions for the
STEVIE KNUCKLES SALUTE

1) Sniff your pits,
with your nose

2) Two thumbs up

3) Wiggle your toes

4) Do the scarecrow

5) Cross your eyes

6) Scissor paper stone

7) Kick a fly

Put it all together
and what do you get?
~~Back ache~~

The Stevie
Knuckles Salute!

Can **Fin** make Prom Night **unforgettable?**
Find out in the laugh-out-loud

Coming soon.

PRESS

Thank you for choosing a Piccadilly Press book.

If you would like to know more about our authors, our books or if you'd just like to know what we're up to, you can find us online.

www.piccadillypress.co.uk

You can also find us on:

We hope to see you soon!